# The World

# of

# Adam Dunne

Tobor Eichmann

For my wife Jelena and sons Darius and Nebo.

The World of Adam Dunne

All that we see or seem, is but a dream within a dream. **~Edgar Allan Poe**

# Chapter

# One

$A$dam rubbed the old scar on the back of his head through his thick black curly hair and stared at the classroom. He looked over at the clock, which seemed perpetually stuck at 2:33pm. The palms of his hands were sweaty as he nervously rolled one over the other as if washing them under invisible water. He looked down at his pants that his mother had bought him from the second hand store, which were now three inches too high. His dark brown colored shoes were one size too big because they were on sale. Droplets of sweat formed on his forehead and down the sides of his face and the words from his mouth were barely audible as he spoke.

"Speak up Adam," said Mrs. Rogers, his teacher who was sitting to the side of him in an armchair.

"Nikola Tesla was born in 1856 in Croatia. He was the father of modern electricity and had many inventions including fluorescent lights, the modern radio, and many types of motors..." Adam continued.

Adam was reciting his oral report, which he had rehearsed for countless hours in front of his father at night. It was a classroom of twenty-two students taught by Mrs. Rogers. She was a short, round woman who wore bright red glasses that seemed out of place against the rest of her dull, colorless wardrobe. She had a reputation for being the strictest teacher in all of C. Ellington Middle School, but for some reason she always showed her rare, gentler side towards Adam. As Adam continued to speak, his mind seemed to disconnect from his mouth and his eyes veered off to the side, through the window of the classroom.

Outside, leaves were falling as the wind billowed through the tall maples in the small town of Somberville, Oregon. One leaf in particular caught Adam's eye. It was a bright red leaf that seemed to take on a life of its own. It strangely went against the wind, briefly lingering in the air prior to landing on the back of a man standing next to one of the tall maples. Adam hadn't noticed the man standing there until now. With an old, tattered waist-high black velvet jacket that was ripped on the right-side pocket, his back was facing the school classroom as if he was looking at something. Adam strained to get a better look at him, but couldn't. He felt as if he had seen this man before, but wasn't exactly sure where. As Adam slowly walked over to the window to get a better look at the somewhat familiar figure, the man seemed to be moving further away without ever taking a step. Adam's head began to hurt. It started slowly from the back of his head, then migrated to just between his eyes. Eventually he reached the window, pressed his nose slightly against it, and held his breath to prevent it from fogging up his view. He tapped on the window, and the man slowly began to turn his head.

"Adam!"

Mrs. Rogers was now standing with her hands on her hips and impatiently tapping her foot on the floor.

Then Adam jolted back to reality. The window had disappeared and he was standing in his original position at the front of the class while muffled giggles could be heard around the room. He nervously gazed around the classroom as the laughter slowly died down.

"Adam, that was very good. You may take your seat now," said Mrs. Rogers.

As Adam slowly walked back to his seat, he glanced back over to the window searching for the mysterious man, but there was no sign of him. On the ground where the man had stood lay a large, bright red leaf.

The rest of the day was a blur and Adam's headache slowly faded, but he couldn't forget the man and leaf. He knew it was just a vision, but it affected him just the same. We wondered if it had anything to do with the bizarre dreams he'd been having. He slowly walked home by taking the familiar block of streets that eventually lead to his house on Pine Street. Having walked the same route for over a month, he could now walk the route blindfolded. He nicknamed each block according to the level of anxiety he felt while walking it. The Blue Zone was the starting point where C. Ellington Middle School was. The next block was the Red Zone, where Adam always felt a bit uneasy because of the scary looking abandoned buildings that lined the street. The Green Zone, also known as the 'Safe Zone' was his own block where his house stood.

As an only child Adam grew accustomed to being alone and found comfort in the solace his own thoughts. They provided a cocoon where he didn't have to worry about the world staring at him and judging him. Leaving the fragile stability of the green zone always made him feel uneasy.

As he walked, he remembered the long talks he and his father would have late at night.  Now that they moved to Melba, Adam loved the talks because they somehow helped him sleep better.

"When you were my age, did you know what you wanted to be when you grew up?" Adam once asked.

"Well," his father answered. "I was always hooked on Science Fiction, so it only seemed fitting that I become an astronaut. As I got older I studied really hard in high school, but your grandparents didn't have the money to send me to college. Oh, I took classes here and there but the years went by. Then I met your mother, we fell in love, and you were born. Before I knew it, the years ticked by and I never pursued it again. Nobody will take a 40 year old beginner astronaut."

Being a tall man with broad shoulders, Adam tried to picture his father cramped into a tiny space capsule.

"Do you ever think about going back to school for it?" asked Adam.

"Sometimes, but then I think about what I would've lost if I had. Choices aren't easy, Addy. But sometimes I still catch myself looking up at the stars."

"So how did you become a warehouse security guard?"

"I kinda fell into it. I worked at the warehouse after high school as a loader and unloader. The warehouse manager thought I was freakishly tall for my age, and because I was a lousy loader, he thought I'd make a better security guard. It was better pay, so I stuck with it even after graduation," explained his father.

Looking at him, Adam thought he fit more as a security guard than an astronaut. He was tall with short black hair and clean-shaven. His mother had always remarked how Adam closely resembled his father with dark brown eyes and square chin.

"What about your accounting class? Are you going to quit your security job if you find a job in accounting?"

"Accounting," started his father, smiling.

"That started as an idea. I was never sure where it would lead."

The World of Adam Dunne

Adam stared into space, seemingly deep in thought. His father sat next to him on the bed and patted his head.

"Why the sudden interest in your future?"

"Oh, I don't know. Today the teacher asked everybody what they wanted to be, and everybody seemed to know except me," answered Adam.

 His father leaned in closer.

"Addy, you're 10 years old. I think you have some time to think about it. I'm sure your friends will have changed their minds many times over before finally settling on what they *really* want to do. Besides, maybe some of your classmates seemed to have it all figured out because they keep getting that question. Maybe they just prepared clever answers.  What I always say is follow your dream and do what you like, but it doesn't hurt if you can earn a living from it, too. I'll bet that a few of your friends from school will end up choosing something they don't like, and at 50 years old they'll wonder where the years went. It'll suddenly dawn on them that they spent almost their entire life chasing someone else's dream instead of their own."

Adam looked as his father who was no longer looking at him, but staring off into space. He wondered if his father was talking about himself. Adam felt sorry for him, because since moving to Melba, his life became nothing but work. On top of that, he began taking morning accounting courses that he'd go to immediately after his night shift. Absolutely exhausted, he would arrive home with barely enough time to eat, sleep for 8 – 9 hours, and then do it all over again the next day. Although Adam only saw his father during these nightly talks, his admiration of him never diminished. His father never once complained about his life or his choices, and he always seemed to have words of wisdom and encouragement.

"I don't have any friends here," said Adam staring at the floor.

"Is that your choice or theirs?" asked his father, looking back at Adam.

Adam thought for a moment.

"I guess a little of both. Whenever I walk by other kids, they seem to stop talking and whisper. I know they're talking about me, but I don't really mind."

"Don't you have anyone you would consider your friend?"

"Not really. Philip was my last friend a year ago before we moved here. I eat lunch by myself while I read my books," Adam solemnly answered.

His father smiled.

"Well, it's good to have friends, even if only one."

"I know," Adam started, "but they're all constantly talking about the latest video games, and I don't play video games."

"You sound just like me when I was your age. If all the kids went left, I went right. Things will work themselves out. You'll see."

Finally Adam reached his house, which seemed like a tiny cottage compared to the larger houses on Pine Street. He unlocked the door with the key he wore around his neck on an old shoestring, unpacked his backpack, and headed for the kitchen. His mother worked at the local diner until around 8pm, but she usually managed to leave food for him to warm up. By the time his mom arrived home, Adam would already have done his homework, washed up, brushed his teeth, and prepared for bed. Since they moved, his father began working the night shifts at King's Shipping. He would arrive late at night to say goodnight if Adam was still awake, which was usually the case since he typically forced himself to stay awake.

At 8:17pm his mother arrived home and came to Adam's room. He always felt sorry for his mother who looked so exhausted when she arrived home. She was a small, almost petite woman with auburn colored hair and a few faint grey strands. He noticed over the past year that her once radiant and glowing smile dissolved, leaving her with a tired and sunken expression on her face. Lately, she had dark circles under her eyes as if she never slept. Over the past year it seemed that her natural spark and glow had faded, leaving the shell of a person that simply went through the motions of life in repetition. She used to grow her hair long, but lately she kept it short. Adam often found auburn strands of hair on the bathroom floor that had fallen out. He wondered if she was sick and his mother and father were keeping it from him.

She poked her head in his room.

"Sleeping already?"

"Nope," answered Adam.

She sat down on his bed next to him.

"How was your day?"

"Okay," he answered shortly.

He didn't want to mention the bizarre vision he had earlier that day because his mother always worried too much.

"Homework all done?" she asked.

Adam nodded.

Normally she would stay and talk to him about his day, but tonight she seemed extremely tired.

"Well, you get some sleep and I'll see you in the morning. Goodnight Addy. I love you," she said softly.

She gently kissed Adam on the cheek, and then stood up and walked towards the door.

"Goodnight mom. Love you," Adam responded while rolling over to face the wall.

She turned off the light as she left the room. Adam started to tell her to leave the lights on so he could stay awake for his father, but tonight he just wanted to go to sleep and forget about this strange day.

He closed his eyes, but could still detect the flickering light across the street caused by the street lamp shining through the overgrown tree. He dozed off for what he thought was not very long, but looked over at the clock to learn that it was now 10:40pm. Adam closed his eyes tighter in attempt to fall sleep faster.

Suddenly a breeze filled the room, which was always a telltale sign that someone had opened the bedroom door. Adam's eyes popped open and he saw his father illuminated by the light in the hallway. Adam sat up in his bed, reached towards his nightstand, and turned the lamp on.

"I was just hoping to catch you before you were asleep. I just wanted to know how the report went," said his father as he walked into the room.

Rubbing his eyes, Adam glanced over at the clock again. To his amazement, it was now almost midnight. His eyes widened in disbelief. This had happened to him a few times before, but this time it was unsettling.

"Addy, you ok?"

"The clock," started Adam.

"Never mind," he continued.

"The report went ok."

"Just ok?" said his father, sitting down on the edge of the bed.

"You spent almost a month preparing for it, and it just went OK? Did you have stage fright, or did you forget something?"

"No, nothing like that," Adam answered.

He didn't want to go into details regarding his disturbing visions. Adam felt that his father was the only one who he felt understood him and he didn't want that to change. He always saw the look of concern in his mother's eyes whenever he talked to her. The only way he could describe it was the way someone watches a fragile egg on the very edge of a kitchen counter about to fall. It was different with his father; Adam cherished the nightly talks. Perhaps it was because of his father's tales of his own boyhood that reminded Adam that his feelings and thoughts weren't that unique.

"It's just that nobody at school seems to be that interested in science," Adam lied.

His father smiled.

"Everybody's built differently. If you had told me that everyone absolutely loved it, I'd know you were lying."

Leaning closer to Adam, he continued.

"Did I ever tell you why I was fascinated with Tesla?"

"Only a million times."

"Ok, this is a million and one," laughed his father.

"Tesla was quirky guy with a lot of things going for him, but everyone thought he was weird. However, that didn't bother him. The other thing I liked about him is that some of his side inventions were made out of *convenience*. For example, if he needed a rare element for one of his inventions that was located only on the other side of the earth, he was the type of person that would just invent a Star Trek transporter to beam himself to that area to get it, without ever considering the transporter invention a big deal."

Listening to his father talk about Tesla's quirkiness made him relate to the scientist, which is why he worshipped his books so much.

Adam's father got up from the bed.

"I should let you get back to sleep, Addy. You look really tired."

Adam laid his head back on his pillow, suspiciously staring at the clock.

"Goodnight dad."

"Goodnight, Addy. Sleep tight."

Adam's father left the room as quietly as he had entered.

Adam switched off the light, still staring at the clock. Before long, his eyes got heavy and he fell asleep.

14

# Chapter

# Two

*A*dam had no use for an alarm clock because he woke up exactly at 7:15 every morning. He brushed his teeth, put on his clothes, and stood staring at his reflection in the mirror. He often wondered if the image on the other side of the mirror had a better life than him.

"Do you have friends there?"

"Do you feel different than everyone else there too?"

He remained standing in front of the mirror for almost five minutes before he walked downstairs for breakfast. As the coffee brewed, Adam's mother was busy making his lunch. She seemed to be thinking of happier times as she blankly stared and smiled. She didn't seem to notice Adam as he sat down at the small kitchen table.

"Morning, mom," he said quietly, not wanting to scare her.

She suddenly snapped out her trance.

"Oh, good morning Addy. I didn't hear you come downstairs. You're quiet as a mouse. Are you hungry?"

"Yes, a little." he answered.

He remembered the times when they all sat down together for breakfast and talked about the plans for the day. Those happier days that seemed so long ago. Since they moved, they never seemed to be together like the good old days back in Melba. His mother seemed to carry the weight of the world on her shoulders, and he often worried about her.

"Did you sleep well?" she asked.

"Yeah, I was dreaming about my old school. It's weird that I always have the same dream. I dream that dad drops me off at school, but I can't find my classroom no matter how long I walk through the hallways. Then some huge, thick wall appears out of nowhere and blocks my path, and I couldn't get around it. That's when I wake up."

"Well, that's some dream! I used to try to look my dreams up in a book your father once got me for my birthday. I finally gave up trying to interpret them because I decided it was all rubbish. Anyway, you better finish your breakfast or you'll be late. Don't forget to take your medicine too."

"Medicine," Adam thought with disgust. It was the worst part of breakfast, but it was ordered by his doctor for his headaches. One oval pill in the morning, and one round one at night. He quickly gulped his breakfast and grudgingly swallowed the chalky white pill. His mother handed him his backpack and kissed him goodbye at the door.

"Love you!" she shouted, as he walked out.

The days were getting brisk and winter was making its coming arrival obvious. Adam walked his daily route to school through the Green Zone, Red Zone, and finally the Blue Zone. As he was crossing the street to his school, the morning bell rang.

"Hi Adam," an almost angelic voice called from behind him.

Adam turned around and saw that the voice was that of Melissa Siegel. Melissa was a 9-year-old girl with long red braided hair that draped over the front of her shoulders. She was almost an inch shorter than Adam. He knew that she sat in the back of the class, but he wasn't exactly sure where.

"I liked your report yesterday," she said.

"My report?" he asked, somewhat confused.

Melissa smiled.

"How many reports did you give yesterday, anyway? I'm talking about your report on that scientist Tesla. I thought it was pretty cool, and stupid me...I thought Tesla was the guy who invented the electric car."

"Oh," started Adam.

"Yeah, a lot of people make that mistake, so don't feel bad. My dad is crazy about Tesla and talks about him all the time. He says if it weren't for the car with his name, he would be one of the most brilliant scientists in history that nobody knows about."

"So what happened at the end?" She asked, frowning.

"What do you mean?" Adam was confused.

"You know, when you kinda zoned out?"

"Oh, I just thought I saw something, but I was wrong," answered Adam, looking away.

He didn't really feel like explaining how sometimes he sees things that aren't there, or the fact that it always seemed to coincide with his headaches. He just wanted to look and feel normal again.

"You've been at this school for nearly two months and you don't talk to anyone. Nobody knows anything about you. You always sit by yourself during lunch reading a book," Melissa continued.

Adam started fidgeting with his hands again searching his mind for a clever reply, but was not successful. Melissa could see that he was starting to look uncomfortable, so she quickly changed the subject.

"So why did you move to Somberville of all places? I heard that you used to live in Melba."

Adam had a look of surprise that she knew this.

"Somberville is not that big and news gets around pretty fast, you know," Melissa explained, as if she had guessed Adam's question.

"It was my parents' idea. I had an accident a year ago and they thought it was best that we move to some place quiet."

"I wouldn't call Somberville quiet. I'd call it practically dead," added Melissa laughing.

"Nobody in their right mind stays here for a long time. You stayed in 4th grade after your accident I guess, so you're the oldest in our class. Was it a car accident?"

"You sure ask a lot of questions," said Adam frowning.

"Sorry. My mom says I'm naturally curious, and that it's good. I've never met anybody that had amnesia before…not for real, anyway. My brother once tried to use it as an excuse for not doing his homework, but it didn't work. So, how long were you in the hospital?"

"I don't really remember," Adam finally confessed, rubbing his hands more intensely now.

"I fell down and hit my head. I don't remember much about it. We never really talk about it."

"How weird! By the way, Halloween is coming up pretty soon. What are you gonna to be?" she asked, trying to change the subject.

"I haven't really thought about it yet. I'm not sure that I'm going to go out. I usually go out with my dad, but he works at night and my mom is usually really tired when she gets home from work."

"What do your parents do? For work I mean?"

"My dad is a night watchman at King's Shipping."

Melissa looked confused. "King's Shipping? Never heard of it."

"My mother works at the Main Street Diner as a waitress," continued Adam.

"Both of my parents work at KCU-TV, you know the local news station?" said Melissa.

"That's where they met. My mom is some kind of editor and my dad does something with computers. He tried explaining it to me many times, but I still don't get it."

Then the second bell rang.

"See you in class!" Melissa said as she disappeared into the crowd, funneling her way into the narrow doorway cf the school.

21

22

# Chapter

# Three

*I*t was a typical start to the day as Adam ritually sat at his desk doodling, as it took his mind off of the dark thoughts he sometimes had.

"Today we're going to start on a class project that should take us well into the holidays," announced Mrs. Rogers.

"It will be a montage of images and stories about the pilgrims that came into America and will lead up to the history of Thanksgiving."

Upon hearing this, Adam looked up from his doodles in amazement. He looked around at the reactions from his classmates' faces, only to find the typical blank stares towards the front of the classroom. He folded up his drawings and placed them in his desk, and before thinking Adam raised his hand.

This caught his teacher off guard as other than the times he was called upon, Adam seldom spoke in front of the group.

"Yes Adam?" Mrs. Rogers said, smiling.

Adam hesitated for a moment as he gathered the words in his head.

"Do we tell the real story or the fake one?"

Looking puzzled, Mrs. Rogers responded.

"What do you mean, Adam?"

"Well, all of the stories about the Indians coming together with the Pilgrims to eat is mostly a lie. There was a freed Indian slave of England named "Squanto" who helped the Pilgrims grow food. He also helped with a peace treaty between the Pilgrims and the Pequot Indians there. They did have a big feast for that, but some of the Pequot tribe didn't agree to the peace treaty, so a war broke out. Later, one of the tribes had their yearly feast and at the same time, some European mercenaries killed about 700 Pequot. After that, they had a celebration for their victory and called it 'Thanksgiving'."

"So," Adam continued, "I guess the pictures will have a lot of red."

Even before the final sentence left his lips, he knew he had done it again. It was just another nail in the coffin of his social awkwardness.

Adam moved his eyes slowly to the left and right as many student's jaws' dropped. He then looked at Mrs. Rogers, whose eyes looked as if they were ready to pop out of their sockets. Without a sound in the room, it seemed longer than ever before someone began to speak again.

Mrs. Rogers finally broke the silence.

"Oh, well, I…I…guess that's one version of events, but I think its best to stick with the official version, OK?"

Adam didn't respond, but instead took his drawings out and covered them with his arm in an attempt to hide them from the view of others.

His father had always told him that people weren't always ready for the truth. He wondered why all the lies were necessary and weren't mentioned at all in the history books.

After Adam's awkward impromptu recital, the day seemed to drag on longer in comparison to other days.  He counted down the minutes until lunchtime. Normally, the lunchroom would be filled with pointless chatter about cool video game strategies. However, today's forecast called for sunny and mild temperatures in the mid 60's, so everyone was eating lunch outside.

Adam slowly walked through the rows of the lunch tables, eyeing groups of kids from grades 5 through 7. He could see that the cliques had already been formed for the year. On the left side were the tables of beauty queens who stayed up to date with the latest fashions and looked down upon those who didn't. Next to them sat the jocks from the little league football team. On the right were the nerds whose membership included hall monitors, the chemistry club, and the chess club. In a normal setting, Adam would probably belong to this group, but he didn't like the idea of being labeled. Instead, Adam chose his usual spot on a lone bench along the school wall. He sat down and began eating the chicken salad sandwich his mother had prepared for him.

As he munched on his sandwich, Adam reached into his backpack and pulled out his book "The Marvelous Inventions of Nikolai Tesla." It was a present from his father when he was seven years old. Although he barely understood a word of it when he first began reading it, he always kept it with him.

Adam's mind began to wander as he pictured himself back in the park in Melba. He was walking and talking with his mother and father about their upcoming vacation to Florida. Adam couldn't seem to remember if his accident had occurred on the way to Florida. He sometimes looked at pictures of palm trees in travel magazines to see if something would spark his memory, but nothing ever seemed to work. Whenever he struggled to remember the events leading up to his accident, his head felt like it was about to explode from pain. Each time he asked his mother about it, she would always give the same answer, "Addy, the doctor says your memory will come back with time and we shouldn't try to rush it. It will come." It had been a year of agony of not knowing what happened and his parents not wanting to discuss it.

Adam's mind switched back to the present just as the bell rang, indicating the end of lunch. Apparently he had zoned out too long, so he gathered up his belongings and began putting his book back into his backpack when suddenly, a shiny red slip of paper fell to the ground. It was thin as tin foil, and it had somehow gotten lodged in his book. He picked it up, turned it over, and saw that it read, "FREAK!" in somewhat crude handwriting. Adam slowly looked around for any visible signs of guilt, but could find no one looking back at him. He crumbled it up and held it so tight that his fist began to tremble. He continued to pack his belongings, along with his unfinished sandwich, back into his backpack and slowly walked back to class.

The rest of the day passed painfully slow. He continued to tightly clench the note in his hand; he couldn't stop thinking about who had written it.

The same questions were circling around in his head.

"How long had the note been there in his book? Was it there since the beginning of the school year, or was it slipped in that same day by one of his classmates?"

The journey home seemed to take even longer these days. The Blue Zone seemed to go on forever, the Red Zone felt like it added an extra ten steps, and he didn't feel any less anxious when he finally reached the Green Zone this time. Finally, Adam reached his house and let himself in. He saw that there was a note left on the refrigerator from his mother.

*"Working a bit later for the overtime. Home at 9. There is meatloaf & peas in the fridge. Love you."*

"Great. Meatloaf again," thought Adam.

This made him think of the school lunch menu that he had to endure whenever his mother was too busy to pack a lunch for him. Apparently someone long ago thought it was a great idea to line up food menus with days of the week, both at home and at school. There was 'Meatloaf Monday,' 'Taco Tuesday,' 'Chicken Wednesday,' 'Mystery Meat Thursday,' and of course, 'Imitation-cheeseburger Friday.' Adam didn't give it much thought. He had more important things to think about, such as analyzing the handwriting from the mysterious note.

Adam's parents always admired his independence and maturity. At the age of five he was able to make his own meals, wash himself, and get ready for bed without being asked. He carefully tiptoed around the house to avoid waking his sleeping father who had to get up in a few hours for his night shift. Adam wished his dad had a regular day job so that they could spend time together like the old days.

After Adam breezed through his math homework, he brushed his teeth, took his nightly pill, and climbed into bed. He picked up the crumpled slip of paper that lay on his bedside table and began to study it again. Finally, he lay back with his head on the pillow as the anger he felt when he first read the note returned, simmering in his mind.

"How dare they? They don't even know anything about me."

He tried to think of something else, but before long his eyes got heavy and he drifted off into a deep sleep.

# Chapter
# Four

**A**s Adam walked through the long hallway, he realized that it wasn't his school in Somberville. It was Studevan Middle School, his old school in Melba. The halls were bustling with students and teachers that didn't seem to notice him.

Suddenly, he began to have the same sinking feeling that he had had many times before. He needed to get to his class before the bell rang, but for some reason he couldn't find it. He hated being late, so he started to panic and began to walk faster.

The crowds in the hallways were dissipating as the individuals went into their classrooms. Suddenly he was alone and a dark figure appeared off in the distance of the hallway. As Adam walked towards the figure, it began to take shape and he quickly recognized the figure to be the man he saw in the schoolyard. He had the same black velvet, waste high jacket with a torn pocket on the right side, but once again, he couldn't see his face. A bright red leaf was on his back once again, but this time it seemed to grow until it appeared to cover half of his back. His hands were outstretched to something unseen, but menacing. He appeared to try to stop it.

Adam was closer now, and called out to the vision.

"Who are you?"

Without answering, the man slowly began to turn around and Adam started trembling with fear.

Out of nowhere, a hand grabbed his shoulder and pulled him back.

"Addy!" a voice called.

Suddenly the image of the hallway and the man broke apart into what seemed like the many pieces of an exploding jigsaw puzzle.

"Addy, wake up!" his mom called out, as she tugged at his shoulder.

"Addy, you were having a bad dream and you're all sweaty. Was it the same dream?" she whispered.

Adam sat up, looked around, and shook his head groggily. He was back in his room. The note he had held tightly when he fell asleep had fallen on the floor. He looked at it, but before he could reach for it his mother snatched it up.

She frowned when she read it.

"What's this? Who wrote this?"

"I.....I don't know. I found it in in one of my books in my backpack. The teacher wants us to start working on a month long project for Thanksgiving. I told her that the real story of Thanksgiving wasn't like a greeting card and I guess nobody liked it."

"What exactly did you say?"

"Its not important. I just wish I would have kept my mouth shut," Adam answered, staring at the floor.

"So you think somebody slipped this note in your book because of your unpopular opinion about Thanksgiving?"

"Of course. I always say the wrong things, but dad told me to always speak my mind and think for myself."

His mom's stern looked dissolved into melancholy.

"Oh Addy, people can be so mean and cruel sometimes. You mustn't take it to heart. You're such a sensitive boy, and I worry about you all the time because of it."

Still clutching the note, she kissed him gently on the forehead and wished him sweet dreams. She then switched off the light on his bedside table and exited the room, leaving the door partially open.

Adam lay in bed remembering his old friends from Melba. They had all gone on to 5th grade, and surely left the memory of Adam Dunne behind. He wondered about the new teacher they had. Was it old Mr. Parks who never seemed to have more than two shirts, or was it young Mrs. Stonebridge who all the boys had a secret crush on?

His thoughts got muddled and turned into random images that meant sleep was tugging at him.

Suddenly there was a delicate creak from the door. It seamlessly blended with Adam's dream about being in his grandmother's old house and the creaky sounds it used to make. Then he heard slow footsteps coming towards his bed. Adam opened his eyes, and in the darkness he could make out the figure of his father standing over him.

"I'm sorry. I didn't mean to wake you," said his father.

"I wasn't sleeping," Adam lied.

Adam rubbed his eyes and switched the light on.

"I understand you had quite a day today," said his father as he sat down in the chair next to Adam's bed.

"Yeah," Adam answered sheepishly.

"Wanna talk about it?"

Adam contemplated making light of the situation, but felt anger again over the note.

"My teacher talked about a Thanksgiving project which is supposed to be the story of the first Thanksgiving. All I did was tell them the story you told me about the Indians being killed, and the new Americans celebrating because of it."

Adam's father stared at Adam emotionless for a moment.

"And why did you tell them that story?"

Looking puzzled, Adam asked, "What do you mean?"

"Addy, I always taught you to think for yourself, that means with your mother and I too.  If we tell you that humans are descended from apes, it doesn't mean that you automatically believe it; you treat it like a theory to prove or disprove. That goes for history too. I'm not saying what I told you about Thanksgiving was wrong, I'm just saying sometimes the truth lies somewhere in the middle."

"But what's the point of history if you can't trust anything they say?" asked Adam, growing frustrated.

"Welcome to the real world, Addy. Asking questions is part of freethinking. Its not that you can't trust anything, but it never hurts to verify. Tesla wasn't brilliant because he went along with the status quo. Besides, reality is not always what you think it is. Healthy skepticism is good. Do you understand?"

"I guess so," Adam answered quietly as he laid his head back on the pillow.

"Ok, get some sleep."

As Adam's father got up and walked towards the door, he turned around.

"I love you, Addy. Always remember that."

He then switched off the light.

Adam's father didn't say these words often, so on the rare occasions that he did say them, it made Adam feel better.

"Love you too, dad. Goodnight."

Adam lay awake in the darkness of his room thinking about the day for what seemed like an eternity.  The anger he felt earlier slowly melted away as he thought about what his father said. He'd always felt different from his classmates, even in his old town of Melba. But for some reason, Somberville made him feel like a total outcast.

Still, there was something else. He could see it in his parents' eyes. His head began to ache while thinking about it. He switched his attention to the light flickering through the window of his room as streetlights shining through the autumn leaves made interesting designs.

Slowly, he fell back asleep.

37

38

# Chapter

# Five

*A*dam woke up the next morning with a cull ache in his head. He tried to remember the strange dream that he had had, but the details were swiftly fading away. He looked over at the window and could see the leaves blowing in the wind. It made him think of the man with the red leaf, which immediately gave him a sick feeling. A feeling of dread came over him as recalled the incidents from the previous day. He wished he could stay at home and read instead of facing his classmates again, and the mysterious culprit who had written the nasty note. He reluctantly dragged himself out of bed and dressed himself.

As he walked down the stairs, the familiar aroma of freshly brewed coffee filled the air. Mom always made sure it was the first thing that she did when she got up. When he entered the kitchen he once again noticed his mother was standing at the sink as she always did. This time he stopped in his tracks. The water was running and he could see the pillars of steam billowing in the air. She stood at the sink scrubbing her hands and looking off to the side with a forlorn look on her face. As the seconds ticked by the scrubbing became more intense and it seemed as if she were trying to remove something that had adhered to her skin. The more she scrubbed, the more distressed her expression became. The scene made Adam anxious and worried.

Not sure what to do, Adam cleared his throat carefully, trying not to frighten her.

"Morning mom," said Adam.

Somewhat startled anyway, she turned around and smiled, nervously. She looked down at her hands, which were now red and raw. She turned the water and almost mechanically she placed scrambled eggs, bacon, and a glass of milk in front of Adam as he sat down.

"Morning, Addy. Did you manage to sleep ok?"

Adam stared at her for a moment with a look of concern, coupled with suspicion.

"Yeah," he answered, not wanting to go into details.

She grabbed a chair, sat down next to Adam, and cupped his hand in hers.

"Addy, I got an email from your teacher. She's concerned about you. She wants to meet with me and discuss something."

Adam looked away.

"Addy, is this about yesterday?"

Still looking away, Adam finally responded, "I have no idea."

"Addy, I'm worried too. Please look at me."

Adam turned to face her, but didn't look her in the eye.

"Addy, this is a fresh start in a new place and I know things are hard, but I need you to understand that you can talk to me about your feelings."

He finally looked at her.

"There's nothing to talk about. Everything's fine. It's not my fault that people aren't freethinkers."

She leaned back in her chair and stared at Adam with a look of concern.

"Where did *that* come from?"

Adam turned his head away again.

"Never mind."

Without another word, Adam took only one bite of bacon, a sip of his milk to take his pill, and got up from the table. He silently walked towards the door and picked up his backpack. His mother walked behind him, grabbed his shoulders, and turned him around. She then knelt down in front of him face to face.

"I love you Addy," she said softly.

"Things will get better. I promise."

She intently stared at him and kissed him on the cheek.

"Have a nice day Addy," she said, trying to smile through her look of concern.

Adam pretended that he didn't notice.

"Bye," Adam said as he left.


Adam closed the door behind him harder than usual and began his trek to school. It was a windy, cold, and drizzly morning in October. Auburn colored leaves covered the rain soaked sidewalk. He pulled his hood over his head to shield himself from the annoying cold drizzle. He could already feel his socks getting wet from the shoes that were developing holes again after being repaired twice. He started to imagine what his old friends in Melba were doing at that very moment. He imagined his friend Philip probably being dropped off at school. Adam's father often took him and Phillip to school together. Only a year had passed, yet to Adam it felt like ages. He pressed himself to remember more of what happened right before his accident. But as usual, the more he tried to think, the more his head began to throb. The doctors said that everyone's brain reacts differently to these types of accidents, but his memory would come back in time. They called it 'Dissociative Amnesia'. "Why can't they just call it 'Amnesia'?" he thought. Whatever the condition, Adam was growing impatient and he wanted answers to the gaps of memory in his life.

He looked up to realize that he had already walked all three blocks to school. He checked the time on his watch and ten minutes had passed; it was already 7:59. He ran to his locker, placed his lunch inside, and hurried to class. As he entered the doorway, he suspiciously looked around to see if anyone appeared mean enough to write the vicious note he found the day before, but no one gave him a second glance. He walked over to his seat and noticed a folded up slip of paper on his chair.

"Not again," thought Adam with dread.

He immediately grabbed the note and sat down.

"Take your seats everyone," Mrs. Rogers said loudly.

As she announced the day's activities, Adam looked down at the note still folded in his hand. He slowly unfolded it and prepared himself for more mental torture that would surely ruin his day. To his surprise, there was a clumsily drawn smiley face. Under the smiley face it read, "Smile, grumpy!"

Adam looked around, and in the back row Melissa sat smiling. He caught himself smiling back. He quickly folded up the note and put it in his pocket. A calm feeling came over him as he began the day's lessons. Maybe it was going to be a good day after all.

The day progressed as usual with Geography, Language Arts, and Math moving at a snail's pace. Finally it was lunchtime. Adam went to his locker to grab his lunch and book on Tesla, and moved to the lunchroom. He found an empty seat at the end of the table of the chess club. He popped open his book and began to munch on his meatloaf sandwich.

He became engrossed with the story of how Tesla made a fortune with his many patents, but he eventually ended up penniless because he wasn't a very good businessman.

"Another book on your favorite superhero?" a voice asked.

Adam looked up and it was Melissa looking down at him, smiling.

"No, it's the same one."

"You either have only one book or you're an awfully slow reader."

Adam smiled.

"Can I sit here?" asked Melissa, pointing to an empty seat across from him.

"Yeah, I guess so."

"So you DO smile. Did you like my note?"

Adam started to answer, but caught himself.

"Wait, which note?"

"The note on your chair, silly. I guess you get so many of them to have to ask," she added laughing.

"No, actually I don't. It was just..."

Adam searched for the right word.

"Unexpected?" prompted Melissa.

"Yeah, that's it."

"You never smile and you're always alone. My mom says to bring people out of their shells, you have to make them smile or laugh."

"Your mom sounds pretty smart," said Adam.

"Oh, she is, but my dad always says I got my brains from him," said Melissa smiling.

"I liked what you said yesterday in class about Thanksgiving," Melissa continued.

"I didn't like the part about the Indians being killed. I just liked that you *said* it. Usually class is so boring, especially history. My mom says they change history all the time because people have such short attention spans and don't remember anything. She says she sees it all the time in her work. She's a news editor for KCU-TV news, you know."

As Melissa spoke, Adam noticed her pearl earrings sparkling in the fluorescent light of the lunchroom. He was fascinated that every turn of her head gave off a different color.

Melissa noticed that Adam appeared hypnotized.

"What?"

Somewhat startled, Adam responded, "Sorry, its just..."

Adam tried to find words that wouldn't make him sound even more strange.

"Tesla had a problem with pearl earrings. They made him go crazy. I don't know why."

Melissa looked at him curiously.

"Are you saying that my earrings are making you go bonkers or something?"

"No, no..." Adam stuttered.

"Its just...I don't know why anyone wouldn't like them."

Melissa smiled at the indirect compliment.

"Well, you can relax anyway. They're plastic."

The more Melissa talked, the more at ease Adam felt with her. She didn't seem to treat him like glass, almost making him feel normal. They both laughed and talked until the end of lunch period before returning to class. The rest of the day was uneventful, until at last, the end of day bell rang. Adam jumped up and walked towards the door in a hurry, trying to avoid eye contact with everyone.

As he walked towards the gate, he saw Melissa talking to a well-dressed woman who was leading her to the parking lot. Melissa turned around and noticed Adam.

"Bye Adam!" Melissa called out.

Adam shyly waved.

The woman glanced at Adam and said something to Melissa. They both turned around to face Adam.

"Do you want a ride home?" Melissa yelled.

"No thanks," he answered while picking up his pace.

Ever since moving to Somberville, Adam was intensely self-conscious because he didn't want anyone to see where he lived. It was a part of his life that he didn't want to share with anyone. He missed his life in Melba. He recalled that they had packed up and moved right after Adam was discharged from the hospital. The memory of that time comes back to him in bits and pieces, but whenever Adam struggled to remember the details, his painful migraine would kick in. It was a subject never discussed at home because any time

Adam would bring anything up about their lives in Somberville, the subject was quickly changed. His migraines started shortly after being discharged from the hospital, which is why he has to take two pills a day. The morning pill often made him nauseous and didn't really seem to help him that much. The night pill made him groggy, and Adam surmised that it might be contributing to his bad dreams.

In the blink of an eye, Adam was standing on his doorstep with no recollection of his walk home due to his deep thoughts about his life in Melba. He reached for the key attached to the shoelace tied around his neck and let himself in.

49

50

# Chapter

# Six

**W**eeks went by and Halloween had come much too soon. Adam tried to scramble for an excuse to stay home, but could find one. She noticed him taking an unusual amount of time to finish his breakfast and finally broke the silence.

"So what's going on today, Addy?"

"It's Halloween," Adam answered, still solemnly staring at this plate.

"I know. The time is just going by so fast."

She noticed a paper bag by Adam's chair and pointed.

"What's that?"

"My costume"

"Really? Are you having a costume party at school?"

"Sort of. It's not really a party, we just dress up and keep our costumes on all day. At the end of the day, each person with the best costume in each class will get a prize."

"Wow, that's sounds like fun. Are you gonna put yours on? I'd love to see it."

Adam pondered for a minute.

"Yeah I guess so, but don't laugh."

"Of course I won't. Hurry. Go put it on!"

Adam grabbed his bag and disappeared into the living room. Moments later, he re-appeared wearing white dress shirt, a thin tie, and his already too-small suit jacket he had received from his grandmother two Christmas' ago, a fake black mustache, and his hair parted down the middle.


She smiled with delight.

"Aww, that's adorable! A little Charlie Chaplin!"

Looking in disbelief, Adam ripped off his mustache.

"Its Nikolai Tesla, mom."

Somewhat mortified, she answered "Oh, well that was my second guess. Honest!"

"No matter. It's still a great costume, Addy. I love it." she added.

She kissed him on the cheek and looked at the clock.

"You better be going, or you'll be late…..Nikolai." she said smiling.

Adam threw his mustache in his backpack and grabbed his coat.

"Addy, since you'll be the first one home tonight for the trick-or-treaters, I'll place the bucket of candy at the door for you to hand out. Or you could just set it outside of the door. Your choice."

The though of him handing out disgusting dollar store bought candy to people he didn't know repulsed him.

He kissed her goodbye and left for school.

Adam was surprised that his spirits weren't dashed by his mother mistaking him for a character from the silent films of the early 1900s. He walked swiftly by the broad array of pumpkins and Halloween decorations posted on the front of the houses in the Green Zone. He picked up his pace when walking through the Red Zone and figured that it really didn't need the Halloween decor to raise the hair on the back of his neck.

Adam reached the Blue Zone when the first school bell rang, as if the school was waiting for his arrival. Off in the distance he noticed what appeared to be an angel looking and waving in his direction. He waited in anticipation for his migraine that usually accompanied these strange aberrations, but to his surprise, it didn't come. As Adam drew closer, he realized that it was Melissa.

"Hurry up! I waited for you because I wanted to see your costume," she yelled.

Adam started jogging and caught up to her, still relieved that it wasn't another hallucination.

"Hi, Adam said, panting.

"Hi Adam. So what are you supposed to be?"

Without a word, Adam opened his backpack and stuck the mustache back on and unzipped his coat.

"Guess."

"Tesla, of course!"

Adam had a look of shock.

"Wow, that's a good guess. Yes."

"Come on, I've seen his picture on your books so many times now. Anybody with a pair of eyes could see it."

"Apparently not my mom. She thought I was Charlie Chaplin."

"Charlie who?"

"Never mind. So you're a princess, right?"

"Close. I'm a fairy." Melissa answered as she waved a pink wand.

"Are you going out tonight? For trick-or-treating I mean."

"No. I don't really see the point." Adam said, staring at the ground.

"Besides, my parents don't allow me to eat a lot of candy, and I'm getting too old for it anyway."

"Well, me too but I still think its fun to get dressed up and go out knocking on doors."

Leaning in closer to Adam, Melissa asked, "By the way, where do you live?"

The question caught Adam off guard.

Just then, the second bell rang.

Adam literally felt saved by the bell. Without answering, he grabbed his backpack and motioned for Melissa to follow him inside the school.


Walking through the busy hallways, Adam made a mental list of the predictable cast of characters. Off to the left there were the superheroes Iron Man, Spiderman, and Superman. Off to the right there were three Princess Leia's, two Wonder Women, and five witches.

Adam and Melissa entered the classroom together and were greeted by a plump woman dressed in black, a pointed hat, a sloppily painted green face, and a fake glued on nose. Adam finally realized that it was Mrs. Rogers dressed up as yet another witch.


The day began as any other day. Adam sat doodling, half listening to Mrs. Rogers as his mind wandered like it usually did at this time of the morning. He imagined being back in Melba with his old friends. He thought about the disturbing visions that he had ever since moving to Somberville and as usual, trying to remember more made his head ache. It reminded him of the first time he rode his new bicycle that his father bought for him when he was five. After removing the training wheels, his father taught him how to ride in an empty parking lot.  Adam seemed to pick it up in no time.  His father had a look of blissful pride as he peddled without help. However, for Adam, it wasn't enough to make his father proud. He wanted to show his father that he was grown up, so he peddled faster.  He could hear his father off in the distance yelling for him to brake, but instead of heeding his father, his peddling became more intense.

It was only a few moments later that Adam lost control and crashed into a curb. He landed on his knee and he remembered seeing the enormous amount of blood before the stabbing pain arrived. His father came running over, and out of breath, picked Adam up and carried him to the car. Adam tried to feel the old scar on his knee through his jeans, remembering how he was more disheartened than hurt. That memory came back to Adam very clear. The pain he felt from trying to remember his accident right before coming to Somberville reminded him of fiddling with the bandage he had on his knee and trying to pull it off.

As Adam pressed himself again to remember his now 1-year-old accident, his head began to ache more. At the same time his scribbling became more intense until his pencil point abruptly broke. The loud sound startled Adam and he was jolted back into the present. When he looked up, Mrs. Rogers had stopped talking and was sternly staring at him. Feeling a mix of embarrassment and guilt, Adam slowly tucked his drawings inside his desk and opened his history book. He could feel the stares from his classmates and dared not to look up from his book to validate his suspicions.

From that point on, Adam was in no mood for any costume contest or even sitting with Melissa at lunch. In fact, he avoided her for the rest of the day. Instead, he found an empty classroom in a seldom-used part of the school to eat his lunch alone.

Adam walked home later at a slower than usual pace. What started out as the most normal day he had had in a while ended in disaster, yet again. He walked into his house and immediately noticed the huge bowl of assorted candy at the foot of the stairs. On the floor next to the bowl was a note.

*"Leave this outside the door for the kids. Leave the light on. See you tonight. Love, mom."*

Adam looked at the huge pile of candy and grimaced. It was 3:15pm; his father was upstairs sleeping and wouldn't be up for another 6 hours at least, so the job was his alone.

"Better do it now," he thought.

Although there was still plenty of daylight left, he grabbed the bowl, set it outside of the door, and switched the light on. He went straight to the kitchen and re-heated the plate of chicken and mashed potatoes his mother had left for him. After eating, he washed up, changed, and started working on his homework.

He was finishing his reading assignments and starting on his Thanksgiving project when he heard laughter outside. He looked at the clock and it was 6:35pm, which meant it was already dark outside. He immediately switched off the light in his room and walked slowly over to the window. Standing behind the sheer curtain, he could see the silhouettes of small figures dressed in capes and gowns. They carried bags up to his walkway, bent down to grab the candy, and then ran away. After the kids were no longer within sight, Adam parted the curtain slightly and spied from left to right. The only source of illumination was the lonely street lamp that was directly across the street from Adam's house. Normally the street lamp gave out light in almost all directions, but tonight the beam was focused like a spotlight for some reason. He watched the masked figures run back and forth almost in slow motion in and out of the light. The movement of the cast of Halloween performers in and out of the spotlight was almost poetic as they kicked up the loose leaves on the street.

Slowly, a form that Adam thought was part of the lamppost became more perceptible as a separate entity and gradually metamorphosed into a tall figure. Upon closer inspection, Adam realized that it was the man with a dark jacket with a ripped pocket on the right side.

"Oh no. Not again," thought Adam, growing anxious.

He imagined that it was some kind of cruel joke played on him by someone. He quickly dismissed the idea since he never told anyone about his visions due to his fear of what people would think of him.

His body was shown in the narrow light of the street lamp and he remained motionless. His face was in the dark, and not visible, but Adam knew the phantom was staring right at him and the feeling made him uneasy. At the same time, like clockwork, his head began to ache. It started from the back of his head and traveled swiftly to the front, right between his eyes.  His vision became blurred and he struggled to keep the figure in focus. This time, Adam thought he wouldn't let go of the vision no matter how horrible the pain became. The people crisscrossed his field of vision and seemed oblivious to the man's presence. Adam remained steadfast in his determination to get to the bottom of this mystery that had been plaguing him ever since moving to Melba. He intensified his stare, as his head felt like it was about to split open.

Without warning, the phantom moved away from the lamppost and began to walk in a slow, fluid like motion across the street towards Adam's house. Adam watched in horror as the dark phantom entered the darkness away from the light and became nothing more than a dark silhouette moving like a bodiless coat flowing in the wind. It reached his walkway with its head still tilted towards the direction of Adam's window.  The light from their door made no difference because it seemed that all forms of light disappeared into a black hole where the phantom's head was. Adam remained frozen in terror as the phantom reached the door. He waited for the sound of someone pounding at the door, but silence remained and Adam could no longer see the figure. His head was now pounding in unison with his heart.

At first, he heard nothing, but as he intently listened, he detected the unmistakable sound of footsteps on the stairs.

"Oh my God. How did it get in??" thought Adam in horror.

"I've got to wake up dad!" He said in a low, trembling voice.

As much as Adam tried to move himself from the window, his fear of facing the phantom now in his own house was overwhelming. He remained at the window as his heavy breath fogged it up with each rapid exhale.

He then heard the familiar creaks of floorboards, which meant that the phantom was just outside of his door. Adam tried to scream but found that his lungs wouldn't utter a sound. Suddenly, he heard the creak of his door and felt a light breeze on his back, which meant the door to his room was now opening. Mental images flashed into his mind about being dragged off into the abyss and never being seen or heard from again. Tears welled up in his eyes at the thought of his parents looking for him all over the house and calling the police in desperation of finding him.

Without warning, a hand grabbed his shoulder. Adam let out a shriek that had been building up inside his lungs, but couldn't get out.

"Addy!" his mother cried.

Adam turned around and his mother was standing in front of him with her diner uniform still on.

"What are you doing at the window in the dark? It almost looked like you were asleep by the way your head was pressed up against it. Are you ok?"

Adam didn't know quite what to say as he was still trembling with fear. She saw the tears in his eyes and pulled him close and squeezed him tightly.

"Oh my God Addy, you're soaking wet! What happened? Were you sleepwalking?"

Adam peered over her shoulder to see if there was another presence in the room, but they were alone.

"I...I..think so," Adam lied.

"Come lie down. I'll make you some chamomile tea to help you sleep."

She walked him towards the bed still holding him tightly.

"I want to wait for Dad," said Adam sitting down on the edge of the bed.

She looked at him sternly.

"Addy, you need to sleep. Lie down. I'll be right back with the tea and your pill."

With that, she left the room.

Adam looked around the room. At this point he was sure he was going mad, but then a thought struck him. Maybe his mother had scared the phantom away. He quickly jumped up and ran to the window. The streets were now empty and the light of the lonely street lamp illuminated half the block again as it always had. He looked from left to right and could no longer see any figures walking around.

"Wait. How could mom be home already?" he thought to himself.

He turned around and looked at the clock, and to his astonishment it was now 9:12pm.

"Mom is right. I must have been sleepwalking," he muttered.

He walked slowly back to the bed and climbed in. He shut his eyes tightly as if to shut out the strange occurrences of that day. While attempting to fall asleep, Adam swore he heard whispers coming from downstairs, but he finally drifted into a deep sleep.

The World of Adam Dunne

# Chapter

# Seven

More weeks flew by as the weather grew colder and the wind began to blow more pronouncedly. The cold air in Somberville seemed to bite with a vengeance compared to what Adam remembered of the fall weather in Melba, adding to his mental list of things that he didn't like about the town. It was Thursday morning and Adam was in a particularly foul mood as he laid in bed. It used to be that he looked forward to the coming weekend, but his nightmares were becoming more vivid and frightening. He had woken up several times during the night in a cold sweat.

"Adam?" his mother called out from the foot of the stairs.

"Are you up yet?"

"Coming!" answered Adam in a monotone voice.

Just then the phone rang downstairs. The phone didn't ring that often and it surprised Adam a bit. He could hear his mother's footsteps downstairs to go answer it. Then there was silence.

Adam swiftly slipped on his socks and pants that he had arranged for himself on the chair the night before. He tiptoed out of his room, careful to avoid the usual creaky areas on the floor. He then slowly eased himself down the stairs as quietly as he could. He could make out a whisper coming from the direction of the kitchen. He mother was on the phone with someone in another one of her 'secret conversations', which seemed to begin shortly after moving to Melba. Adam reached the bottom of the stairs and started towards the kitchen. The whispering became clearer.

"I just wanted to escape. I wasn't thinking clearly……"

"I know. I know it's wrong….."

"It's been so long but I'm not sure we're ready even now…."

Who was his mother talking to? Adam walked slowly closer to the kitchen in the hopes of solving the mystery. His mother was turned sideways, but she caught a sight of Adam in the corner of her eye and gasped.

"Adam!"

"I have to go. Everything's fine. We'll talk later," she told the mysterious person on the phone and hung up quickly.

"I...I..didn't see you there," she said as she turned back to Adam.

"Are we in trouble? What's going on?" asked Adam impatiently.

She searched for words, not knowing how much of the conversation Adam overheard.

After a few seconds she finally spoke.

"No, Addy. We're not in trouble. It's just some problems I was discussing with some of my co-workers at the diner. We think we're treated unfairly, and some of them are thinking of quitting..."

Her voice shook as she spoke, and she seemed to be making the story up as she went on.

"Its really nothing to be concerned about," she said finally.

Adam knew she was lying, but he didn't press her on the matter.

He sat down at the table in front of his eggs, orange juice, and morning pill and simply stared.

"I'll be visiting your school during my lunch hour today," she said.

"I'm just having a chat with your teacher."

Adam's stomach sank at this news because his teacher will no doubt reinforce the fact that he's peculiar and says peculiar things. He had hoped that the situation had blown over regarding the Thanksgiving saga by now.

"OK," answered Adam.

"I'll be going right back to work, but if I see you at lunch I'll stop by and say hello."

Adam cringed at the thought. He didn't need any more attention brought to him than he already had. He took a few bites of his egg, put his pill in his mouth, and took a gulp of orange juice. As he got up from the table, his mother placed her hand on his.

"I know things look dark right now, Addy. Things will get better. I promise."

She seemed to utter these words more often these days, so often it seemed liked she was trying to convince *herself* of it. However, this time was a bit different, there was genuine distress in her voice. What was she really going to discuss with his teacher? Did it have anything to do with the mysterious stranger on the other end of the phone?

Adam said nothing, withdrew his hand from hers, and walked towards the door. As he picked up his backpack and opened the door, he thought he heard a soft sobbing, but he wasn't sure and didn't bother to look back as he closed the door behind him.

*Green Zone.*

The events of the morning put Adam in a worse mood. Usually, his mind was able to drift far away on his walk to school, but this time each step seemed to take him farther away from school. All of his fears came rushing back to him at once. Who wrote the nasty note? How had they slipped it into his book without him noticing? What will his teacher say to his mother? Surely she was still fuming over his graphic dissertation of Thanksgiving. Different scenarios of that conversation entered his mind.

*Red Zone.*

Adam shook off the bad thoughts and focused on his path. Off in the distance he noticed a tall, dark figure walking in the same direction in a smooth, fluid-like motion. Adam strained to get a closer view, but the figure was too far to make out any detail. He picked up his pace in order to get a closer look, but the details of the figure remained out of focus. Desperate to get closer view Adam started a s ow jog. As the image began to come into focus his head began to ache. There was no mistake; the moving image was t1e man with the red leaf, which seemed to defy gravity as it clung to his back. He had the same black velvet waste high jacket with a torn pocket on the right side. Despite the throbbing in his head, Adam pressed on forward determined to expose the phantom that haunted him relentlessly.

*Blue Zone.*

Adam was now a stone's throw away from the figure. He started to call out, but he caught himself because he wasn't sure if he was mentally prepared for the face of this apparition. Almost half a block away now, Adam slowed down. His head was splitting and the pain was unbearable to the point that he had to hold his head on both sides in a vice grip to stop the pounding.

*Even closer.*

The figure crossed the street and Adam was close behind. From the corner of his eye, he saw a fast moving object coming in his direction from the right as he stepped out into the street. The blaring of the car's horn and the screeching of the tires sent Adam tumbling backwards to the ground in shock. The smell of burnt rubber filled the air as a heavy set man quickly opened the car door and ran over to Adam as he sat dazed and confused on the ground.

"Are you ok, young man?" the man asked, almost out of breath.

Adam looked around and saw that the phantom had again disappeared.

"Yeah, I'm ok. Sorry. I guess I wasn't watching where I was going."

"Well, you should be more careful. I could have killed you, young man." the man said helping Adam to his feet.

Just then, the first school bell rang.

"I have to get to class. Sorry again, Sir!" Adam yelled as he dashed off towards the main entrance of the school, noticing that his migraine had disappeared.

# The World of Adam Dunne

# Chapter
# Eight

*A*dam's mother sat in an empty classroom, impatiently tapping her half-painted chipped nails on the desk. She glanced at her watch and compared it to the clock on the wall. It was 12:10pm. She heard the sounds of laughter outside as the students were talking and playing. She walked over near the window to see if Adam was visible, but she didn't see him anywhere. She pictured him sitting alone, still sulking over the conversation earlier in the morning.

Suddenly, the door behind her opened and there stood Mrs. Rogers.

"Hi Mrs. Dunne. Thank you for coming."

Adam's mother walked back to a student chair and sat down.

Mrs. Rogers sat in adjacent chair and turned it around to face her.

"Mrs. Dunne....."

"Linda," Adam's mother interrupted.

"Please, call me Linda."

"Ok, Linda. I'll get right to the point. Adam is one of our brightest students here at C. Ellington. However, I am a bit concerned about him."

Adam's mother looked on with anxiety wondering where the conversation was leading.

"He's alone most of the time. He rarely speaks in class…."

Adam's mother interrupted again.

"Mrs. Rogers, I know what you're getting at. Adam is a quiet boy. He's intensely shy. We've also had very hard year as you know…."

"Its not that, Linda," Mrs. Rogers interjected.

She reached into a manila folder, pulled out a stack of papers, and laid it on the desk in front of Adam's mother.

"I found these in Adam's desk. Adam likes to doodle in class. In fact, he's quite an artist. But it's the *pictures* that he draws. I'm no psychologist, but to me this looks like a cry for help."

She picked up the drawings. The first drawing was an image of a dark, ominous figure in a cave-like hole with menacing red eyes peering out. The opening and walls of the cave looked as if Adam had made continuous circular motions almost to the point of tearing the paper. She flipped through the drawings, as each next drawing appeared more sinister than the previous. The drawings appeared to show a mix of fury and utter despair, which made her stomach sink. Tears welled up in her eyes as she placed the drawings back on the desk and pushed them aside.

"What have I done?" she sobbed.

Mrs. Rogers reached over and put her hand on top of hers.

"I know your history. I know it's been incredibly tough, but if I were you I would seriously consider getting him help."

Adam's mother gazed out of the window, deep in thought. Finally, she turned back to face Mrs. Rogers.

"You're absolutely right. I've known this for a very long time, but I just couldn't face it. It's time."

"Thank you," she said as she gathered up the drawings and put them in her purse.

She got up, walked towards the door, and then turned around.

"We're not bad people," she said with tears in her eyes.

Before Mrs. Rogers had a chance to respond, Adam's mother left.

She walked to the end of the empty hallway and stopped. She stood with her back against a locker and began to cry.

After a while the bell rang, signifying the end of lunch. She wiped her tears, looked at her watch, and realized that she had ten minutes to get back to work. She walked hurriedly towards the exit against the flow of students returning from lunch. She strained her eyes to see if Adam was among them, but she didn't see him anywhere. She then quickly walked out of the door towards her car in the parking lot.

Adam appeared from behind a door where he was hiding and watched her get into her car and drive away.

For the remainder of the day, Adam had a sick, worried feeling in the pit of his stomach. He tried several times during that day to see if he could get a hint from Mrs. Roger's demeanor, but she didn't give any visible clues. He walked home with a feeling of dread of what the evening would bring.

Adam usually breezed through his homework in no time, but tonight he struggled to keep his focus on his

Geometry. It was 6pm Thursday night, and he sat staring at his blank worksheet. What did his mother and Mrs. Rogers talk about? He had struggled to see his mother's mood in the hallway while staying hidden from view, but couldn't. He imagined that his opinion about Thanksgiving caused such uproar that he had been expelled, but this thought didn't seem like such a bad punishment to him.

After fumbling through the rest of his homework, Adam took his pill, washed up, and headed for bed. He always walked quietly so that he wouldn't wake his father that had to get up for work in just a few hours. Sitting in bed, he stared at his Tesla posters on the wall that were starting to lose their adhesion and curling. Before long he heard the sound of keys in the front door. He quickly switched the light off and got under the covers. He could hear his mother walking downstairs, and then opening the closet door to put her coat away. There was a momentary silence and Adam imagined his mother gazing up the stairway into the darkness, listening for movement. He then heard the creak of the stairs, so he closed his eyes and covered his head as he heard his mother reach the top of the stairs. She slowly opened the door, and Adam slightly opened his eyes and could see the thin sliver of light that crossed him from the hallway. Without warning, his mother switched on the light.

"You know, it's strange. I could see that your light was on from the street, and now suddenly you're asleep. That's so bizarre."

Feeling caught in his unspoken lie, Adam pushed the covers away from his face and sat up in his bed, squinting at the bright light.

"I was awake," Adam admitted.

"Addy, I haven't been fair to you. In fact, it's shameful. I know you have a lot of questions and have had them for quite some time. I've been soul searching and trying to figure out who I'm actually trying to protect."

Adam didn't know quite how to respond, but listened anyway.

She sat down on the bed and faced Adam.

"I've made a decision. I was able to get someone to cover my shifts this weekend and I was thinking that we could drive to Melba to see your grandmother, and maybe your old friends."

Adam sat straight up with excitement.

"You mean it?"

"I sure do," answered his mother smiling and wiping away tears.

It had been over a year since he had seen his old friends and neighborhood. When he got out of the hospital, Adam's family moved six hours away to Somberville immediately.

"I'll pick you up from school with your bag packed, and we'll get on the highway. We'll be driving all night, and should get into Melba late tomorrow night. You'll probably sleep most of the way."

By the smile on his face, she could tell that he approved.

"Now get some rest. We have a big day tomorrow," she said as she pulled the covers up to his chin.

She got up and walked over to the doorway.

"I think it'll be good for all of us," she said switching off the light.

Adam lay back in bed almost too excited to sleep.

He then thought he heard whispering coming from downstairs. Looking over at the clock illuminated in the dark, it was now 9:17pm. It was usually the time that his father started stirring around, preparing for his nightshift.

Adam could then hear the soft tiptoes up the stairs, which usually signified his father's ritual of telling him goodnight before leaving for work. The door then opened and his father walked in, switching on the light.

"I didn't have a chance to ask how the Thanksgiving project is working out," glancing at paper cutout Indians and pilgrims Adam had on his desk.

"Fine."

"So do you need any help with any part of it?"

"Not really. I'm almost done. Guess I'll have to pretend I don't think for myself."

His father chucked.

"I know. Your mother and I always thought about homeschooling you, but time was always the problem."

Adam saw that his father's face suddenly grew serious.

"Big day tomorrow," he said as he sat down in the chair next to Adam's bed.

"Yeah, mom says you guys will pick me up from school tomorrow and we'll be in Melba sometime tomorrow night."

His father didn't answer. Adam's excitement drained from his body, as he knew what his father's silence meant.

"You're not coming, are you?" asked Adam suspiciously.

"I'm sorry Addy."

Adam began to tear up.

"I hate your job, and I hate your classes! Why can't it be like the old days?" shouted Adam.

"Addy, things change. My love for you and your mother is something that won't. You have to understand that. I know it's not easy to understand now, but someday you will."

Adam didn't answer. Instead he stared at the wall poster of Albert Einstein his father once gave him.

"Adam?" his father whispered.

"OK, you don't need to answer."

Adam lay back, thinking with his head on his pillow. His father got up to give him a kiss on the forehead, but Adam turned his head to the wall to avoid it. Instead, his father leaned back and switched off the table lamp. Adam listened as his father's footsteps grew fainter, leading to a dead silence. He felt guilty for blowing up at this father, but decided that he would apologize after the weekend.

# The World of Adam Dunne

82

# Chapter

# Nine

$A$dam woke up the next morning, still a bit shaken from the nightmare that he had just had and still sulking, but couldn't immediately remember why. He looked over at the clock and it was 7:15. There was something that he was supposed to remember about today.

"We're going back to Melba!" he finally realized.

He got dressed and dashed downstairs. Mom was in her usual spot at the sink in the kitchen as the smell of freshly brewed coffee filled the air.

"Morning mom," said Adam.

His mother turned around and smiled. As he sat down, she placed a plate of scrambled eggs and bacon and a glass of milk in front of Adam.

"Morning, Addy. Did you manage to sleep ok finally?"

"Well," Adam started," I kinda waited until dad showed up to say goodnight, because I could hear you guys whispering. He told me he's not going with us this weekend! Why didn't you tell me?"

His mother stood back and stared at Adam with a look of concern.

"Adam, please. We have a great weekend planned. Don't do this now. We can talk about it later. Now eat your breakfast. Your lunch is in your backpack. I put an extra apple inside."

Adam finished half of his breakfast, took a sip of his milk with his pill, and got up from the table. He walked towards the door and picked up his backpack, still brooding. His mother walked behind him, grabbed his shoulders, and turned him around. She knelt down in front of him face to face.

"We're going to see grandmother. She hasn't seen you in such a long time and she will be so happy to see you."

"Ok, I have to go," said Adam averting his eyes to the door.

She kissed him on the cheek.

"Have a nice day dear. I'll pack your things and wait for you outside in the school parking lot."

"Ok, bye mom." answered Adam has he left.

Adam slowly walked to school as he thought about his grandmother. It was his mother's mother, and Adam often wondered why they didn't visit after the move. After the accident, she got sick and had to move to another place where a lot of old people live, but she refused to sell her house. His grandfather, or mother's father, died just a few years ago, and his father's parents before he was born.

Adam struggled to pay attention to Mrs. Roger's monotone way of speaking throughout the day, but he managed as best as he could. It didn't help that his nightmares often made him groggy, especially after lunch. As the day was cold, he ate his lunch inside next to Melissa as she told him about her favorite movies. Adam wasn't interested in movies, but because *he* was not the subject matter, he listened. The rest of the day was thankfully uneventful until the end of day bell finally rang.

"Don't forget class, next week we'll start putting our Thanksgiving montage together!"

Adam didn't dare look up at her as she brought the subject up. He quickly grabbed his backpack, walked out of the classroom, grabbed his coat from the locker, and ran out towards the parking lot.


Melissa somehow managed to beat him outside and he called out to her.

"Melissa, I forgot to tell you that I'm going away for the weekend to Melba with my mom and dad."

Adam couldn't believe his words that he blurted out, but it was too late.

"That's great!!"

"I guess you'll get to hang out with your old friends," responded Melissa.

Adam shook his head nervously.

"Who's this, Melissa?" asked her mother as she walked up.

"Oh, this is Adam Dunne. I was telling you about him. He's new in my class," answered Melissa.

"Oh, yes. Nice to meet you, Adam. I'm Leslie, Melissa's mother," said Mrs. Siegel as she held out her hand to shake his.

"Adam moved here from Melba and he's going back there for the weekend."

"Well, that sounds like fun," Melissa's mother said as she smiled.

"Adam, there you are!" called out Adam's mother as she approached them.

"I was looking for you."

"Hi mom," said Adam, still nervous from telling his half-truth about his father going.

"Guess we should go," he said as he took his mother's hand trying to coax her away.

"Is this your one of your classmates?" his mother asked, looking rudely at Adam.

"Uh, yes… I'm Melissa," said Melissa holding out her hand.

"And I'm Leslie, Melissa's mother."

"Linda….Dunne," said Adam's mother in return.

Melissa's mother thought for a moment.

"Linda Dunne. Have we met before?" she asked.

"I don't think so. I can never make it to the parent-teachers' meeting because of my schedule."

"You seem really familiar to me. It will come to me. We probably passed each other in the mall or something," said Melissa's mother.


Adam tugged on his mother's coat

"Mom, we need to go. Traffic, remember?"

"Well, you guys better go. Adam tells us you have a big weekend planned," said Melissa's mother.

"We sure do. We're going to my mom's place in Melba. Adam hasn't seen her in a while."

There was an awkward silence.

"I guess Adam's right. We better get on the highway to beat the traffic. It was nice meeting you," she added as they turned to leave.

"You too!" answered Melissa's mother.

"Bye Adam!" she added.

Adam waved to Melissa and she waved back in what seemed like slow motion as Adam and his mother continued to their car.

They sat in their parked car when she turned and looked at him disapprovingly.

"Well, that was pretty rude, young man. You don't want me to meet your friends?"

"You mean *friend*," said Adam.

"Well, you have to start somewhere and it looks you chose a very pretty girl to be your first. Her mother seems nice. We need to meet more people here. Maybe we can invite them over sometime?"

Adam looked down. He didn't know how to tell her that he was embarrassed of his shabby home or his unwillingness to let anyone into his 'world'. As they made their way onto the highway, Adam looked back at the small town of Somberville, wondering if it would ever feel like home. His mother noticed the lost look on his face.

"What's on your mind, kiddo?"

"I'm thinking about our old home, and seeing my old friends and grandma again," answered Adam.

"Adam, as I told you a lot of things have changed. Your grandmother's mind isn't what it used to be. Right after the….accident last year your grandmother had a stroke. Do you know what damage that can do?"

"Not really," answered Adam.

"Well, it usually causes problems for people moving and speaking afterwards because that part of their brain is damaged. Your grandmother has both problems, which is why she's being cared for in a special home. I try to talk to her almost every day by phone, but most of the time I can't understand her. Sometimes when people have this kind of injury it's difficult for them to speak. They may think they are saying one thing, but it comes out a tangled mess and it's pretty frustrating for them. Her short-term memory is bad too. I did tell her that we're coming but I don't know if she will remember."

She sighed.

"I wanted to stay in Melba, but with everything that happened, it was just too much. I felt really guilty about leaving her, but if I had stayed I probably would have had a stroke myself. Now, she's getting the best care possible."

His mother kept looking over at Adam as if trying to make herself feel less guilty.

"Your father always talked about getting out of the city for a quieter life, and this seemed like the best solution for us. We're going to see your grandmother, but we will be staying at her old house."

Her expression now changed and she looked more serious.

"Addy, the doctors suggested that we go back to the old neighborhood, to familiar surroundings, so that we could gently jog your memory as to what happened. It has to be *your* journey. Understand?"

Adam nodded.

"We're also going to meet with a kind of specialist for your condition. She's going to talk to you and see what you can remember. "

Adam gazed out of the window as the farm fields and small towns whizzed by. It was a cold Oregon fall day and the ground met the sinking sun that was surrounded by a red sky in a blazing battle. Eventually the sky surrendered and it became dark.

She reached over, opened her purse, took out a small plastic bag of Adam's pills and a bottle of water, and handed it to him.

"Here, take your pill, close your eyes, and try to get some sleep," she said.

"We still have quite a long drive ahead of us. We'll be there in the middle of the night and after we unload, we'll get some proper sleep. Tomorrow morning, we'll go to see your grandmother. Besides, you've been looking pretty tired lately. I know you're not sleeping well because sometimes I hear you yelling in your sleep."

"It's my dreams," Adam started.

"They're getting scarier and scarier."

"Still having the dreams about that wall?"

"Yup."

Adam wanted to tell her about the strange man with the leaf, but decided not to.

"Maybe this so-called 'specialist' can talk to you about your dreams. We have an appointment with her on Sunday."


Adam looked at his mother curiously.

"It sounds like you don't like her already."

"No, don't get me wrong. I'm all for it if it will help you," explained his mother.

"I'm just not crazy about the idea of tinkering around with a person's brain."

Adam continued to stare out of the car window.

"Now, put your head back and try to take a nap."

Adam put his head back against the headrest. The highway lamps streamed by like shooting stars. Before long, despite his attempts to keep them open, his eyes became heavy and he drifted off to sleep.

Soon, Adam was transported to a different place and time. He stood at the fence that separated the school grounds from a vast open field of trees that used to have auburn colored leaves, but the trees were shedding their leaves, leaving bare branches. The man was again standing near one of the only trees where a multitude of red leaves remained. He turned towards the tree and slowly raised his arms as if to protest the falling of the leaves. All of the sudden, thunder clapped and Adam looked up at the sky, but there was nothing other than clear blue as far as the eye could see. Where had the thunder come from? A bright red leaf that swayed in the wind finally shook its hold from the tree's branch and floated in the air. Adam watched the bright red leaf as it searched for its final resting place, finding its way onto the man's back. Adam tried to call out to the man, but to his surprise there was no sound. In fact, there was no sound anywhere. It was like watching the scene unfolding from behind soundproof glass. In order to get the man's attention, he tried to scream at the top of his, but it was no use. He grabbed the fence and began to shake with all of his strength, but the man gave no indication that he was aware of Adam's presence.

Suddenly, he heard a sound from behind that sounded like someone shuffling through leaves. At first it was very faint, but it slowly became closer and louder. Being too terrified to turn around, he clenched the fence even tighter until his fingers became numb.

"Adam," a familiar gentle voice called out.

"Adam it's me," the voice repeated.

Adam slowly turned around. To his surprise, it was Melissa with her flowing red hair that seemed to blend in with the color of the trees.

"Melissa?" said Adam in a startled voice.

"What are you doing here?

"I've come to tell you something. You must come with me," Melissa answered in an almost divine voice.

"But you don't understand. I have to know who this man is!" he answered motioning to the direction behind him.

Melissa peered over his shoulder.

"What man?"

Adam turned around, and to his shock, the man had once again disappeared. On the ground where the man had stood lay a bright red leaf. He turned back to Melissa and tears formed as he began to speak.

"I don't understand what's happening!"

Melissa softly stroked Adam's thick curly black hair.

"You have to walk to through the tunnel to get to the light."

Melissa reached out her hand.

"Come with me."

As the sky grew darker and the landscape around him became distant, Adam reached out to hold Melissa's hand, but she was suddenly out of reach.

"Adam?" his mother spoke softly while gently nudging him.

"Adam, wake up. We're here."

Adam sat up in his seat and rubbed his eyes. Parked in the driveway, they had finally made it to his grandmother's house on Elmer Street.

Adam felt his headache had returned with a vengeance.

# Chapter

# Ten

**A**s Adam's mother unpacked the car, she handed him two grocery bags of food she had packed from home.

"Here, help me with these bags."

It was 11:12pm and the neighborhood was silent. They walked through the garden that led to the front door. Adam noticed the swing that his grandfather used to push him on was still hanging from branch of the old overgrown oak tree. Further to the right lay a stone birdbath on its side, with no sign of water ever being inside. The lawn looked as if it hadn't been cut since they moved from Melba. As they reached the front door, his mother put the bags down and searched in her purse for the house keys. Adam noticed that the door's red paint had peeled so badly that it was difficult to see what color it had once been in the dim light. Finally, the door was open and they stepped inside. She found the light switch on the wall, praying that the electricity worked. The lights came on, and thin strands of old spider webs dangled from the single hanging light fixture in the hallway.

The air had not been disturbed for over a year, leaving a distinct musty odor.

"Well, thank God the bulbs still work," she said with relief.

"Why don't you go put this stuff in the kitchen while I get the rest of the bags?"

Adam picked up the bags of groceries and headed for the kitchen. The walls were still covered with his baby pictures and pictures of relatives he had either never met or was too young to remember. There were also pictures of his mother and father on their wedding day. His mom was in a long white silk gown, and his father was dressed in a black tuxedo with black bow tie. He sported a mustache that he had shaved off since the wedding. Adam always noticed how happy and carefree they looked in that picture. By feeling his way along the wall in the dim light coming from the living room, he reached the kitchen and turned on the light. There was a thick layer of dust covering everything. He groaned as he imagined what the bedrooms looked like.

After some time, his mother returned with all the bags from the car.

"Wow, I guess the maid is on vacation," she said jokingly.

"Let me get a fire going and I'll make us something to eat."

Adam's head still hurt, and food was the last thing on his mind.

"I'm not really hungry," he said.

"Are you sure? We have some cold sandwiches…" his mother started.

"Nah. I'm just really tired, and my head hurts. I wanna go to bed."

"Ok, you'll sleep in my old room. Let me just run up and change the sheets. They're probably just as dusty as the furniture," she sighed.

With that, she took the two small suitcases upstairs. Adam walked out of the kitchen and into the living room. All of his grandmother's things were still in the same place, just as he remembered. They always seemed to have the biggest collection of souvenirs from their many trips. There were mugs from their trip to Florida, dusty snow globes from their trip to Austria, and even a red Dala horse from their trip to Stockholm, Sweden. Adam dusted off a spot on the plastic covered couch and sat down. His head was starting to feel a bit better when his mother called out from upstairs.

"Addy, your bed is ready!"

"Coming!"

He got up to walk towards the staircase when he heard a low scratching sound. He stood motionless to see if he had imagined it, but after a few seconds he heard it again. It seemed to be coming from the direction of the dining room. He walked slowly and silently towards the sound and found that it was coming from the door to the basement. He thought it sounded like a cat trying to scratch its way out, although he knew his grandparents never owned a cat. He thought perhaps it was a stray cat that had somehow found its way in and made its home in his grandmother's abandoned house. Adam slowly reached for the door. His heart started to race as he suddenly had the thought that maybe it wasn't a cat at all, but maybe more phantoms haunting him. He withdrew his hand, leaned closer, and placed his ear against the door. The scratching suddenly stopped. Had he imagined it as he did the man with the red leaf?

"Addy, where are you?" his mother called out.

"Coming!"

He backed away from the door, looking at it suspiciously. "I'll investigate it tomorrow," he thought to himself.

Adam's mother's old room was filled with old dolls that his grandmother never wanted to throw out. On the walls were posters of music bands he had never seen or heard of. On the dresser were pictures of his mother in her younger days in high school. A few of the pictures were of her cheerleading squad. As if it were yesterday, Adam recalled how his grandmother never missed the chance to brag about it. A fresh set of sheets was on the bed. His mother put his suitcase on a white satin covered chair in the corner and laid out his pajamas out on the bed.

"I opened the window to let a bit of fresh air in here. The air is so stale! Close it if you get too cold, OK?"

"OK," he answered.

Adam sat down on the bed rubbing his head.

"Headache's back?" she asked.

"Yup."

She walked over and sat down beside Adam and put her arm around him.

"I think you just a need a good night's sleep. You were tossing and turning in the car. Tomorrow you'll be as good as new. We'll go see grandma around noon, but on the way we'll drive right through our old neighborhood. Would you like that?"

Adam simply smiled.

"Ok then. I'll tell you what. We'll skip the teeth brushing tonight. Just change into your pajamas and go right to bed, OK? Are you sure you won't eat anything?"

He shook his head no in response.

"Alright, I'll be back to say goodnight," she said.

She got up and switched on a small bedside table lamp. She then switched the ceiling light off, leaving the room with a soft red glow from the table's red lamp shade. Adam stared at the lamp for a while as his mom looked around the room at her old things.

"Mom never changes anything in this house. It's exactly the way it was when I was growing up, and even after I moved out."

Her words seemed like she was complaining about it, but when he looked up at her she was smiling as if having good memories. Then she seemed to switch back to the present.

"OK, you change and I'll be back."

With that, she disappeared through the doorway. Adam undressed, put on his pajamas, and climbed into bed. He lay there staring at the soft red glow on the bedroom walls and gradually closed his eyes. When his mother returned nearly five minutes later, Adam had already fallen fast asleep. She pulled the covers up to his neck and kissed him on the forehead. Then she stood back and stared at Adam for a moment with slight look of worry. Finally, she silently walked out of the room, leaving the door slightly open.

# Chapter
# Eleven

*A*dam awoke with the sun beaming on his face. He blinked a few times, and initially didn't know where he was. But after a few seconds it all came back to him. He looked over at the window as the curtains moved back and forth from the crisp November air. He could hear traffic down on the street below. He didn't remember falling asleep the night before. In fact, he didn't remember anything after he laid down last night, but he a felt relief that it was the first night in a while that he didn't have bad dreams. "Maybe mom was right after all. I needed just to get away so the bad dreams would stay away," he thought. Adam got out of bed and found the floor to be freezing. His grandmother had always hated carpeting, and the bare floors made the house feel even colder. He tiptoed out of the room to his grandmother's room where his mother was sleeping, but the bed was empty. At that moment, he heard a tune coming from downstairs. At first it was low, but as he leaned over the bannister to listen more carefully, he realized that it was his mother singing. From the wonderful smell, he figured that she was in the kitchen making breakfast.

"Mom?" he called out.

"Down here!" she answered.

Adam walked down the stairs and joined her in the kitchen.

"Good morning sleepy head," she said as she turned around.

"I was about come check on you. It's not like you to sleep this late, even on the weekends."

Adam looked around for a clock and found one next to the refrigerator, which read 10:10am.

"You were exhausted last night, so I just let you sleep. How are you feeling?" she asked.

"I feel better, but I'm starving," he answered rubbing his stomach.

"Well, I'd be shocked if you weren't. You didn't have dinner last night," she said, placing breakfast in front of him.

Breakfast consisted of scrambled eggs, ham, orange juice, and his usual pill. Without a word, Adam stuffed his mouth with a fork full of ham.

"Slow down mister before you choke," she said.

Adam took a drink of orange juice and thought for a moment.

"Mom, did grandma ever own a cat?"

"No, never," she answered. "Your grandmother hated cats. She thought they were God's punishment on man for his sins, or something like that. Why?"

Adam turned around and looked back at the basement door.

"I thought I heard scratching like a cat last right coming from the basement door."

"It could be this old house. Houses like this are always settling on their foundations and they make weird noises. I used to think the house was haunted," she said.

Adam's eyes widened.

"But it wasn't of course. There's nothing down there but old furniture and some old things that we stored here before we moved. But just to be sure no cats made their way through a hole, I'll check it out."

She looked at her watch, and it was now 10:30am.

"I promised the people at mom's retirement home that we would be there by lunchtime so that we could have lunch with your grandmother. Finish your breakfast, wash up, and change. It's about a 30 minute drive," she said as she got up from her chair.

Adam and his mother sat in the parked car outside of the house as she looked at her watch again.

"Addy, here's the deal," she said. "The plan was to drive by the old neighborhood on the way to see your grandmother, but now it's a bit late. We'll have to swing by on the way back or possibly tomorrow."

Adam thought for a moment.

"It's not a big deal. I just wanted to see if Philip was still around. He was my best friend. The rest were what we called *accessories*."

She laughed.

"You got your weird humor from your father. Well then, after leaving the retirement home, I'll call Philip's mother and tell them that we'll stop by tomorrow. By the way, I checked out the basement and...surprise! No cats! I also checked all the windows, and there's no way any cats could ever make it in. Therefore, it is my professional opinion that you heard the house settling."

She then started the ignition and they drove away.

Adam and his mother drove the local roads leading out of the city in route to Cedar Retirement Home, which was on the edge of town.

"Does grandma have the same kind of injury that I have?" asked Adam.

"No, your grandmother has something completely different. The only thing in common was that it happened around the same time as your accident, and both were caused by trauma," she answered.

"What do you mean, trauma?" he asked.

"That's when something terrible happens to you, and it can cause harm to your body or mind, or both. As I told you, there's nothing wrong with your grandmother's long-term memory. I'm still trying to figure out if that's a good thing… at least for me," she said.

Adam looked at her oddly.

"What do you mean?"

"After everything that happened last year, we just packed up and left. I feel like I should have been there for her, but I just couldn't stay."

She looked at Adam with glassy eyes, almost as if seeking approval.

"Do you understand?"

Adam nodded.

"Now remember," she continued, "she won't be able to communicate that well with you, but she will understand."

Off in the distance Adam saw the top of his father's old workplace, Littleton Shipping.

"Look, there's dad's old job over there!"

Without a response, he looked back at his mother, whose gaze remained focused on the road. Without warning, Adam started to feel dizzy and a bit nauseous.

"Mom, I don't feel so good," he said holding his stomach.

"I think I'm getting car sick."

She looked over and noticed a few beads of sweat forming on his forehead. She slowed down and pulled over on the side of the road.

"Let me open the window," she said calmly.

Coming to a full stop and opening window on Adam's side, she felt his forehead, which felt cold and clammy.

"My, this was all of a sudden. You've never gotten car sick before."

She looked down and rubbed her forehead.

"Maybe this was a mistake coming here. Maybe it's too soon."

Adam wondered what she meant, but he felt too woozy to ask.

"Just breathe. It'll pass," she advised.

He breathed deeply, and after a few minutes his head started to clear. As soon as Adam felt better they started the car and continued on their journey to Cedar, only a bit slower for the remainder of the drive.

They made it to the facility at 11:20am. Adam saw that it was a huge, stately building surrounded by tall trees. They entered the lobby and his mother went straight to the sign-in desk.

"Hello, may I help you?" asked a woman at the desk, barely looking up from her book.

"Yes, we're here to see Amelia Johnston."

"Are you a relative?" the woman asked.

"Yes, I'm her daughter. There should be a note that I'm visiting today."

The woman finally looked up from her book with a surprised expression.

"Oh, well then....I'm sure she'll be happy to see you," she said, with an almost sarcastic tone.

"They're just sitting down for lunch. Do you know the way?"

"Yes, I do," she answered.

She took Adam's hand and walked down the long corridor, which was darker than Adam had pictured. He thought it smelled like a mixture of mothballs and cleaning supplies. The carpet was old with a design that probably looked nice a long time ago, but lost its appeal with age. Finally they reached the end of the corridor and stood at the entrance of a large room filled with seniors sitting at round tables who instead of eating, just sat staring into space. At each table sat a nurse helping to feed them. Adam felt sad witnessing the depressing sight of so many old people that looked so unhappy and lost. She searched the room for her mother when she finally spotted someone with silver hair, dressed in a beige shawl, sitting with her back to them. She sat facing a large window looking out over the garden. One of the nurses sat next to her.  Adam felt his mother's grip tighten as she pointed to the far left corner.

"There she is," she whispered, pointing.

They slowly walked toward grandmother, but when they reached the middle of the room, his mother stopped.

"Pull me Adam, or my legs won't move," she whispered again.

Adam pulled her further to the last ten steps.

"Hi mom," she said with a shaky voice.

The nurse looked up at her and smiled.

"Looks like you have a visitor, Mrs. Johnston."

Adam's grandmother slowly turned her head and looked up. Adam immediately noticed that his grandmother's face had somehow changed. He had always loved that she always looked happy, with a sparkle in her eye. Now, the sparkle seemed to have disappeared and her face was somewhat distorted. Adam's mother pulled one of the chairs next to his grandmother and took her hand as she sat down.

"Mom? It's me, Linda. Do you remember we talked on the phone about us visiting? "

First, Adam's grandmother had a look of surprise, but slowly it was replaced by a look he had never seen on his grandmother's face. It was a look of anger or hate that gave Adam chills. Then she pulled her hand away and turned, facing the window again.

"Addy's here, mom," she said, trying to salvage the situation.

Then his grandmother quickly turned back around to them as Adam stepped forward.

"Hi Grandma," Adam said nervously.

The nurse got up from the table and said, "I'll leave you guys alone for some family time. If you need anything, there's a buzzer on the table that will alert the nurses in the kitchen."

With that, she patted Adam's grandmother on the shoulder and walked away.

Adam's mother pulled up a chair for Adam and he sat down next to her. Usually when he saw his grandmother he would run and hug her. This time it was different. He wasn't sure how to act, so he felt very awkward. His grandmother looked into Adam's eyes and tears began to form as she opened her crooked mouth trying to speak.

"Add...Add...Add...," she kept repeating, quivering her mouth.

Adam tried to hide his shock of her condition, but it was too much for him. He began to sob. Then he got up out of his chair and put his arms around her.

"Add...Add...Add...,"she continued repeating herself, wrapping her left arm around Adam's shoulder and pulling him closer.

From the corner of his eye Adam could see his mother quietly crying with her face in her hands. They remained in that position for some time before his mother finally broke the silence.

"Mom, there's so much I want to say and I don't know where to begin."

Adam's grandmother released her hold on Adam and he sat down, still holding on to his grandmother's hand.

"I wanted to visit but I just couldn't. I had our bags packed for a very long time, waiting for just the right time, but I always made up excuses not to get in the car. I was simply too scared. The memories would just come rushing back to me and I would think "Not yet.""

Adam listened intently to what his mother was revealing, because he hadn't heard this version before. She looked over at him and noticed that he was listening closely.

"Adam, let me talk to grandma alone for a minute, OK? You can take a walk in the garden outside, but stay where I can see you."

Adam stood up slowly and started to walk towards the door to the garden, but then turned back and grabbed his grandmother's hand.

"I'll be back grandma. Don't worry. We'll all be back to visit you more often."

Adam stared down at the floor as he spoke.

"Dad had to work, so he couldn't come with us this time. But I'll make him come next time, I promise."

Adam felt his grandmother grip his hand more firmly as if acknowledging his words, then the grip became tighter and a bit uncomfortable. Adam looked up and saw that his grandmother's eyes were wide and fixed on him almost as if in terror. He had never seen this look on his grandmother's face, and it frightened him.

"Add... Add.. Add... Not...Not...Not...," she uttered incomprehensibly.

Adam looked down at his hand, which was now in pain.

"Grandma, you're hurting me!"

"Add…Add..Add…Not…Not…Not…," she repeated louder.

Everyone in the dining area turned around to see what was going on. Adam's mother jumped out of her chair and grabbed her hand to release the death grip she had on Adam's.

"Mom, let go! You're hurting him. Please!"

Without warning, his grandmother released Adam's hand and he fell backwards. He got up quickly and terrified, and ran out into the garden.

He walked slowly through the garden with the thoughts of what just happened running through his mind. What's wrong with her? Is this what happens to people when they have strokes? What was she trying to say? Adam found a bench in the garden across from the big window of the dining room where he could see his mother on her knees next to his grandmother's chair, talking to her while stroking her hand. A nurse was on the other side with a very concerned look on her face. His grandmother didn't seem to be answering. Instead, her eyes were intensely locked on Adam. Adam's mother looked up and saw him through the window. She then kneeled closer to his grandmother saying something else. She pointed to Adam several times while talking emotionally about something, then Adam realized that *he* was the topic of the discussion. What had he done? What were they talking about? At this instant he was conflicted. He wanted to leave, but he also wanted to be with his grandmother. He wanted also to stay in Melba in the hopes of feeling normal again, but now even his grandmother was treating him like a freak.

After some time his mother motioned for him to come back inside. Adam sat there for a moment wondering if his grandmother had calmed down and if he should go back inside. Then he noticed that she had fallen asleep where she sat at the table. He walked back inside the dining area and stood in front of his mother.

"The nurse gave her something to calm down, and it looks like she fell asleep. Let's take her back to her room. We'll munch on something quick in her room if you're hungry," his mother whispered.

Adam agreed.

They grabbed a few pre-wrapped turkey sandwiches from the buffet table, then wheeled his grandmother to her room at the end of the long hallway. A nurse followed closely behind guiding them. Finally, they reached room 22A, his grandmother's room. They quietly opened the door and wheeled her in. She opened her eyes only once as the nurse helped her into bed. Seeing Adam, she smiled, murmured something, but instantly fell back asleep. After the nurse left, Adam's mother turned to Adam.

"I'm sorry Adam. I told you that grandmother was not well."

"You were talking about me. What were you talking about?" Adam interrupted.

"What do you mean?" she asked, trying to avoid direct eye contact.

"Mom, tell me the truth! What's wrong with me

"You're right Adam. It's so unfair to you," she said at last with a deep sigh.

"Do you remember me telling you that we're going to meet someone who will help you remember your accident?"

Adam nodded.

"We have an appointment with her tomorrow. She's coming to the house and she's going to help us, she will help you remember."

Adam clearly wasn't satisfied with her answer.

"But grandma knows something. She was trying to tell me something."

"It's hard to say what your grandmother knows, but please believe me… we only want to help you. Now, I have an idea. Why don't you stay with your grandmother and read one of your books like you used to do? I'm going to go talk to the staff here and see if we can take her out her tomorrow… OK?"

Adam knew that she was clearly trying to change the subject yet again, but decided to drop it. He sat down on the floor and looked over at his grandmother.

"She's sleeping. What's the point?"

"Addy, please."

"OK."

She turned and left the room quickly. Adam reached into his backpack and pulled out one of his books on Tesla and began to read aloud.

"Chapter 1: Nikola Tesla was born in 1856 in Croatia…...."

116

# Chapter
# Twelve

**B**y the time Adam's mother returned to the room it was 3:15pm, and the sun's little warmth outside was starting to give way to the coming cold evening.

"She's still sleeping, huh?" she asked.

"Yup," Adam answered while munching on an apple.

"Mom, am I going to end up like grandma? I mean, she has something wrong with her brain and so do I."

His mother closed the door to the room and sat on the floor in front of Adam.

"No, Addy. I don't want you worry about that. As I told you, you and grandma have two completely different issues. Because of her stroke she has problems talking and moving. You had an injury to your head last year that made you forget some things, that's all."

She could see that Adam still looked troubled.

"I know there's a lot of things going on that you don't understand. Listen, I talked to the administrator. We can take grandma out tomorrow, so I was thinking I could come back here alone early tomorrow morning and bring her back to the house. Dr. Hansen, the psychologist will be stopping by at 11:30am, and we should be back by then. She's very good at what she does from what I'm told, and she helps people remember things. I'll make breakfast and leave it on the stove for you. How does that sound?"

"What about visiting Philip?" Adam asked.

"We'll have plenty of time to visit him before we head home. I forgot to tell you that I did call his mom and he's excited that you're back in town."

Adam seemed to perk up with this news.

She looked down at her watch.

"It's almost 3:30pm. I think we should get on the road back to the house."

Adam finished his apple and started packing his backpack.

"I'll just write a note for the morning staff to remind grandma that we'll be back tomorrow morning," she said.

Before they left the room, she turned off the ceiling light and turned on the small bedside table lamp. She bent over and kissed grandmother gently on the forehead.

"See you tomorrow grandma," whispered Adam hoping that she could hear him.

He took his mother's hand as he closed the door behind them.  Together, they walked to the main desk.

Adam's mother scribbled a note and handed it to the nurse.

"Can you make sure that the morning staff gets this?" She asked one of the nurses.

The nurse examined the note and smiled.

"Sure thing, Mrs. Dunne. See you tomorrow," answered the nurse.

As they walked out of the building, Adam tried to think of anything to take his mind off of what happened with his grandmother. He thought of his old neighborhood and the possibility of seeing Philip the next day. Philip was his best friend, although they never actually talked about it. It was a friendship that developed in spite of their differences. In fact, Adam didn't really like Philip that much at the beginning, but was asked by Philip's mother to come to visit as a 'good influence.'  Adam thought Philip was always full of himself. He always boasted about unimportant things, such as the newest iPhone that his father bought him for his birthday. Over time, however, they became good friends and were practically inseparable. He remembered that one of their more amusing games was coming up with new insults for each other as a greeting. However, after coming up with 'Nimrod' one time, Adam suspected that Philip cheated with a dictionary.

Compared to Adam, Philip was never particularly great in school. Adam thought that Philip tried to copy his behavior many times, which he always thought it was a bit weird. On several occasions Philip would borrow some of his Tesla books that he would return unread, complaining that he didn't understand any of it. He had an older brother in high school, but Adam hardly ever saw him when he visited, except for when he came home briefly to eat. Adam had met Philip's father only once since his parents were divorced. The one time that Adam did meet him, he remembered there was a terrible argument with him and Philip's mother, and Philip didn't seem the same for a long time afterwards. Adam was always curious about his friend's father, but he didn't think that asking Philip questions was a good idea. Maybe some things are better left alone.

Adam's thoughts turned back to his grandmother. She had always been a strong willed and outspoken person who didn't take any guff from anyone. When she entered a room, her presence was known and everyone respected her. She had always been protective of him for as long as he could remember. His earliest memories of her were before his school years when his father would drop him off at his grandmother's house on the way to work; he would spend the entire day with his grandparents' place playing. Adam was always getting into mischief because he was so curious. His grandfather sometimes jokingly called him 'George,' after Curious George. He always had the most fascinating things in the small bedroom that was repurposed as a study. His grandfather was a retired Navy officer and collected shiny coins from all over the world. Although the room was off limits to him, Adam would often play with an old telescope and sextant that his grandfather kept in his desk drawer. He was caught red handed a few times spying on the neighbors with the telescope through the window. "What have you gotten yourself into now, George?", his grandfather would say after catching him in the act. Rather than punish Adam for touching things that were off limits, his grandfather would sit down with him and teach him how to use them properly. Of course this was always followed by a lesson in asking permission first.

When Adam was five, he skipped pre-school at the advice of all of his parents' friends and went straight to first grade. "He's so advanced and independent for his age," they would say. He remembered his first day like it was yesterday. Adam stood in front of the mirror staring at himself in his new clothes. He didn't like the way the pants felt because they were too scratchy. He still had the bandage over his knee from his bicycle fall, and the pants seemed to pull at it. His stomach felt as if it was going to drop and he wondered if it was the same feeling actors felt before they went on stage for the very first time. He had never been away from his parents or grandparents, completely on his own with strangers before, and the thought of it made him dizzy. On the first day, his grandmother walked him to school for what seemed to be the longest, most dreaded walk at the time.

He had often rode by in a car, so when they finally reached the school, Adam realized how much larger and intimidating the building seemed. He walked into the classroom, still holding his grandmother's hand tightly, and the first thing that he remembered seeing was a tall pole with an American flag in the corner. All the kids sat in groups of six with their desks pushed against each other, reminding Adam of small beehives. They sat with crayons and blank images on paper, all seeming to look up at Adam in unison. As Adam stood in the doorway alone, his grandmother walked over to the teacher and whispered something. The unrelenting stares from the other kids made him extremely uncomfortable and exposed, so Adam compensated by staring at the floor. Finally, the teacher and his grandmother motioned for him and Adam slowly walked over.

"Hi Adam. I'm Mrs. Weckerle. Welcome to the class. There's an empty chair next to the boy over there with the striped shirt," she said, pointing to an empty hive chair in the center of the class.

"Class, I'd like you to meet Adam Dunne," Mrs. Weckerle announced.

"Hi Adam,"they all responded, almost robotically.

Adam looked over at his grandmother, who said nothing as she smiled. He walked over to the empty seat and could feel the eyes monitoring him with each step he took.

As he sat down, the boy in the striped shirt leaned over and whispered, "Hi. I'm Philip."

"Hi. I'm Adam," Adam whispered back.

"Yeah, I kinda got that," he said chuckling.

Adam's grandmother whispered a few more things to Mrs. Weckerle and blew a kiss to him as she left the room.

Adam remembered that it was one of the most dramatic changes in his life at the time. However, he and Philip grew to be best friends over time and Mrs. Weckerle turned out to be the kindest, most patient teacher he had had to date.

124

# Chapter

# Thirteen

*T*he sun was setting in Melba as Adam and his mother drove down the lonely local roads back to his grandmother's house. Adam tried his best to keep his eyes closed for most of the trip so that he wouldn't get sick again. She looked over at him several times with a worried look on her face. Throughout the ride, she tried to make small talk to take Adam's mind off of the day's dramatic events.

"Grandma's new home looks pretty nice, huh?"

"Yup," Adam answered, still keeping his eyes closed.

Actually, Adam didn't picture such a sterile place as his grandmother's new home. Up to that moment he imagined his grandmother spending a short time there, recuperating before returning home. He suddenly began to realize how many things had changed since he left Melba, and how they would now never be the same.

It was dusk when they finally pulled in front of the house. Adam got out of the car first and immediately walked to the middle of the garden. He bent down, picked up the birdbath, and made it upright. His mother said nothing, but smiled and put her arm around him. Together they entered the house.

"Buuuuurrrrr, it gets cold in here in no time at all," said Adam's mother.

"I'll start a fire and get dinner ready while you unpack your things."

Adam unpacked his things and sat at the dining room table thinking about the events of the day. He scratched at the patterns of dried water streaks on the table where his mother had tried to clean the dust away the night before. After some time, she came over with two plates of food. It was mashed potatoes and something that looked like chicken. He looked at the plate expressionless, which she noticed right away.

"Hey, don't give me that look. It's the best I could do. I just grabbed what was in the fridge at home and wrapped it up."

"No, it's fine."

She then reached down underneath the table for something.

"Look what I found!" she said, pulling out an old stack of photo albums.

"Oh no. Not old pictures again," Adam sighed. "Every time I come to grandma's she brings out these old pictures and makes me stare at them for hours. Now *you're* doing it."

"I like looking at these old pictures because I get nostalgic," she answered.

As she flipped through the first album she began to narrate each page. Adam tried his best to pretend he was interested, even though the photographs all looked the same to him. In the beginning, there were mostly old and faded photographs of people that Adam never met. The later photographs were in color and Adam finally started to recognize some of the faces. There were pictures of his mother with pigtails and missing teeth when she was about his present age. There were also photos of the day he was born, with his father holding him while wearing his white security guard uniform.

"Your father looks so proud in that picture. His boss was so despicable. He wasn't a nice man. Your father had to go back to work right after you were born, but your father never complained because jobs were hard to come by in Melba at that time."

She often complained about the boss at the factory and how unfair he had treated all of the employees. She also didn't like the odd hours that kept his father away for most of the day and part of the night, but it was the only shift available. Adam never once heard his father complain about his job though; he always seemed to see the bright side of everything. After moving to Melba, his father had started accounting classes and Adam suspected it was his mother's idea. The hours at his new job in Melba combined with the accounting classes made things even tougher.

Adam looked at the picture again. He remembered his father wearing the same uniform when he picked him up from school; the same one he wears today. He liked going to his father's job and doing the rounds with him before sitting down in his office to do his homework. After some time of looking through the entire collection, she looked up at the clock.

"Oh boy, where does the time go?"

It was already after 6pm, so she cleaned up the table and sent Adam upstairs to wash up, change, and take his pill.

After coming downstairs and spending a few minutes in front of the TV, Adam's eyes got heavy and he began to doze off. The fire his mother started in the fireplace felt warm and cozy, and he didn't want to move from the couch. She walked by and saw him half asleep, so she poked him on the shoulder.

"Hey, I guess it's time for bed, sleepy head."

"Yeah, yeah," Adam responded, groggily.

His body felt like it weighed a ton as he peeled himself from the plastic covered couch, which left a sweaty outline of his body. He had always hated those couches because they were easy to sit on, but almost impossible to get off of. Adam walked up the stairs like a zombie, went into his room, and collapsed onto the bed. His mother followed him and jokingly remarked at his condition.

"My, you're tired."

"It must be the chicken. I know you're poisoning me," responded Adam smiling.

"Thanks for the compliment on my cooking, wise guy," she continued, laughing.

She moved him over and pulled back the covers for him.

"You know, you're getting too old for me to tuck you in."

Adam just smiled without answering. She bent down and kissed him on the forehead.

"Remember, we have a big day tomorrow. If I'm not here when you wake up, don't panic. I'll be off to pick up your grandmother, but I'll leave your breakfast on the stove….OK ADAM?" she asked, raising her voice so that he could hear her better.

"OK."

With that, she turned off the light and left the room.

Adam thought about how in some hours his father would be waking up in Somberville to an empty house, getting ready for his night shift. Adam felt bad for him. He also realized that there would be no nightly talk to lift his spirits that night.

130

He briefly watched the trees outside as they were illuminated by the yellow street lamps and moved in the night breeze, and fell asleep.

# Chapter Fourteen

*A*dam woke up the next morning to sirens blaring through the street. At first he thought it was part of his dream, but then he sat up and realized that it was fire trucks speeding by. "I hope mom didn't set the house on fire with the fireplace," he thought. He looked at the tiny clock on the nightstand and it was 10:30am.

"Mom?" Adam called out.

There was no answer. "What did mom say last night? Oh yeah, she went to pick up grandma and breakfast should be on the stove." He recollected. Adam put his feet on the cold floor and shivered. Wearing only shorts and a T-shirt, he grabbed the blanket, wrapped himself in it, and tiptoed downstairs. All the curtains were drawn closed, and the house was quiet and dark.  When he entered the kitchen he saw the note from his mother:

*"Eggs and ham on a plate in the microwave. Just press the timer for 1 minute. Should be back by 11. Love you!"*

Adam opened the microwave just to check and make sure before pressing the timer.

As he watched the microwave digits count down, he felt a sense of dread at the thought of seeing his grandmother again. Was she going to scare him again? What upset her in the first place? When the microwave dinged, Adam took his breakfast out and walked over to the dining room table, which had a single pill waiting for him. He was hungrier than he realized as he began to eat his eggs in bug chunks and take his pill.

He looked around the dining room. Other than the dust, everything was just as he remembered from the last time he visited his grandmother's place. The huge china closet off to the left still had old dishes and knickknacks that he was never allowed to touch. He remembered the times where he snuck into the china closet and 'borrowed' two small plates and glued them together because they made the perfect flying saucer. His grandmother had discovered the plates hidden under the bed he was sleeping, and he was grounded for a week because of it. If his grandmother has seen the amount of dust that had accumulated now on the cabinet she would not be pleased, he thought.

As he was thinking about what to say to his grandmother when she arrived, he heard something. It was a low scratching sound coming from the door of the basement. Adam stopped chewing, turned around, and stared at the door. The scratching sound continued, but got more intense as if whatever was on the other side knew Adam was listening.

"Shoo, go away cat!" cried Adam in a loud voice.

But the scratching continued. He looked down at the eggs and ham on his plate.

"Mom said she checked for cats but didn't find any. It must have come back in when it smelled the food," he thought.

He quietly stood up and with the blanket sti l covering him and picked up a small piece of ham from his plate. Then, slowly, so as not to make any floorboards creak, he tiptoed over to the door. He put his ear against the door as the scratching continued. He reached for the doorknob, but as soon as his hand touched it, the scratching stopped.

"What kind of weird cat is this?" He thought.

He couldn't stand it anymore. He had to know what was going on behind the door. Finally, he quickly turned the knob and yanked the door wide open. A blast of cold air hit his face. It smelled like a mixture of dust and mold. Adam looked down, and to his shock, there was no cat. He looked at the back of the door and saw no scratch marks either. With the blanket still around his shoulders and the piece of ham still in his hand, Adam decided he needed to know what was down in the basement.

He found the light switch on the wall to the right and flipped it on. A dim light appeared somewhere down in the basement. He stood still for a moment, looking for signs of movement, but there was none. He took the first step down the long staircase leading into the basement. The old wooden stairs seemed colder than the floors in the house. He slowly crept down the stairs, carefully looking at every dark shadow for any sign of a cat.

"Here, kitty kitty," he called out.

Finally, he made it to the bottom of the stairs. The concrete floor was dirty, making him feel stupid for not wearing shoes. He had always hated going down in the basement at his grandparent's because it was constantly cold and damp. He even imagined spirits that lived in the house centuries ago haunted it.

"Too much television," his grandmother would say whenever he mentioned his fears.

Adam looked around and saw the same dusty old furniture that had been there every time he visited. There were old paintings stacked up against the wall and myriad of boxes with old books. He stooped down to look under the old furniture, thinking maybe the cat was hiding there, but there was not. When he stood up, something to the left of him caught his eye, and he saw something move slightly.

"Aha," he thought.

He moved some of the boxes aside and slowly walked over to the other side of the basement. He wasn't exactly sure where the movement came from, or if it was real, or his mind playing tricks on him again. Adam stood motionless, holding his breath while listening and watching from side to side. Suddenly, off to the left, something moved again. It was accompanied by a creaking sound. He moved quickly but silently towards the direction of the sound. He finally reached the source and realized that the creaking sound was coming from a portable clothing rack. Adam recognized his mother's clothes hanging on the long rack. They were pushed to one side as if someone was trying to make room for something else. At the end of the rack hung a dark garment that swung back and forth as if someone had just disturbed it. He walked forward trying to get a closer look.

Suddenly Adam backed away in horror, dropping the piece of ham he had been holding. It was a black velvet jacket with a ripped pocket on the right side. It was the same jacket worn by the man in his dreams that haunted him almost every night. Adam rubbed the old scar on the back of his head and shook his head to make the vision disappear.

"No!" he screamed. "NO NO NO NO NO NO!!! WHAT DO YOU WANT FROM ME? LEAVE ME ALONE!"

Adam dropped the blanket to the floor. He fell to his knees and started sobbing. Suddenly, he felt a hand on his shoulder. Startled, Adam screamed.

"Adam? What's wrong? What happened? What are you doing down here?" a voice shouted.

He looked up and saw his mother standing over him. She helped him to his feet and held him close as he continued to cry uncontrollably. He raised his armed and pointed to the clothes rack.

"There. The jacket. It's in my dreams! It belongs to the man with the red leaf that I keep seeing! And now it's here! How did it get here??"

His mother looked up at the jacket. She looked back at Adam and knelt down holding Adam's face with both of her hands.

"Addy, that jacket belonged to your father. There's nothing to be afraid of."

Adam looked at her in disbelief as a feeling of rage slowly boiled up inside of him.

"Why are you saying that? That's not dad's jacket! Why would you say that?"

"Because it's true," answered his mother softly.

"He used to wear it before we got married, and I always nagged him to throw it away, but he refused…"

"STOP IT!" interrupted Adam.

He held his hands against his ears to muffle the sound of his mother's voice.

She pleaded.

"Addy, you have to listen to me! Addy, please! Addy! ADAM, YOUR FATHER IS DEAD. DO YOU HEAR ME? YOU HAVE TO SNAP OUT OF THIS!"

When she realized what she blurted out, she hung her head low and tears filled her eyes. Adam removed his hands from his ears. His eyes widened and his mouth opened as if he attempted to scream. His body suddenly felt limp, and he slumped over into his mother's arms.

138

# Chapter

# Fifteen

"**A**dam? Adam, can you hear me?" a distant voice called.

Adam opened his eyes. At first, everything was fuzzy. He could see the dark outline of three figures sitting around him, but didn't recognize them right away. He blinked his eyes several times until they slowly came into focus. His grandmother was sitting to the left of him trying to smile with her eyes squinted. His mother was sitting to the right of him, holding his hand with an intense look of concern on her face. Directly in front of him was a face he didn't recognize. She had long, straight black hair and wore rectangle-shaped glasses. Adam was lying in one of his grandmother's reclining chairs with a cold, wet towel on his forehead. He tried to sit up, but the woman reached her hand out to push his arm.

"Relax Adam, you're okay now," she said. "My name is Dr. Hansen, but you can call me Mary. How do you feel?"

"I feel a bit dizzy. What happened?" asked Adam, holding the towel against his forehead.

Before anyone could answer, the events played back in his mind like a movie. The basement, the missing cat, something moving, the clothes rack, the jacket from his dreams, and finally the terrible news about his father.

"Addy, you passed out in the basement and I carried you upstairs." said his mother softly.

"It's true, isn't it? Dad died," said Adam, answering his own question.

"When did he die?"

His mother pulled her chair closer to him and cupped his hand with both of hers.

"Addy, your father died over a year ago."

Adam stared at the ceiling wide-eyed, trying desperately to absorb what his mother was saying.

"Right now there's a lot you don't understand, Adam," said Dr. Hansen.

"Think of your mind as a bridge that's broken in the middle, preventing the cars from passing. I'll try to help you fill in that gap by helping you remember. Some of the memories will be painful, but it it's the only way for you to heal. Do you understand?"

Adam shook his head slowly.

"Good."

She then reached down to the floor and unzipped a black leather bag. She took out a glass bottle containing what appeared to be some type of gel. Adam had never seen anything like it before.

"What's that?" he asked.

"This is a Lava Lamp, Adam," she answered softly.

"We'll use it to help you relax."

She plugged it in. Adam thought it was the most interesting thing he'd ever seen. There was what appeared to be a blob at the bottom, but when the doctor switched it on, the entire glass became illuminated with a soft blue color. She gestured to Adam's mother to close the curtains. The room became black as a night except for the soft blue glow coming from the lava lamp.

"Adam, I want you to try to relax every muscle in your body and focus on the lamp," she said with a softer voice leaning forward.

"I'm going to take you back to a year ago. I'm going to be with you the entire time and you'll be my tour guide. Relax and focus on the lamp."

Adam focused intensely on the lamp. At first he didn't notice anything special, but after a few minutes he began to notice strange shapes forming in the gel. It reminded him of watching jellyfish, but in slow motion. Soon there was nothing else in the room besides Adam, the lamp, and the doctor's voice.

Doctor Hansen: Adam, I'm going to count backwards from five to one. When I reach one, you'll fall into a deep sleep, but you'll still be able to hear my voice.

"OK."

Doctor Hansen: "Don't be afraid. Your mother and grandmother are here beside you. Just relax and listen to my voice."

"Your body is becoming lighter and you feel yourself floating weightlessly in the deep blue glow...."

"Here we go: 5...4...3...2...1."

Adam closed his eyes and found himself in total darkness. He could feel the weight of his own body gradually melt away and the feeling was indescribable. He gazed into the darkness and could make out the faint outlines of his mother and grandmother sitting off to the side.

Doctor Hansen: "Adam, take me back to September of last year. Take me back to the beginning of the school year. What do you remember?"

At first Adam said nothing as his eyes rapidly darted back and forth under his eyelids. He then smiled.

"I'm in my old school."

He grimaced.

"It's hot. I don't like the heat. They don't have air conditioning in most parts of the school. It's Thursday of the first week of school and I'm talking to Philip. He's telling me about his trip to Ohio and I'm bored listening although I pretend that I'm not. We're not supposed to be talking in class and I think Mr. Thompson just saw us."

Doctor Hansen: "What did you do after school?"

(Smiling) "I'm outside of school waiting for dad. Wow. it's really hot. I hate standing in the sun, but if I don't dad might not be able to spot me."

Doctor Hansen: "This is an exciting day. Why?"

"Dad is picking me up during his break and we're going to get ice cream. Then I'm going back to the warehouse with him. It's a secret because he's not allowed to have breaks outside and he doesn't want mom to know I'm eating ice cream before dinner.

Hmmm..I think I'll have one scoop of mint and one scoop of vanilla."

Doctor Hansen: "Tell me about the warehouse visit Adam. Describe what you see."

"I'm sitting in dad's office. Everybody at dad's job is gone for the day. I just finished my ice cream and starting my Geometry homework. The air conditioning is on too high and there's no way to turn it down. It's always so cold here.  Dad's complaining about the TV news again."

"What's 'propaganda' dad?"

"Dad sees that I keep looking at it so he turns it off."

Doctor Hansen: "What happened then, Adam?"

"It's quiet. It's always quiet at dad's job after everybody leaves. I have to start on my book report on Thomas Jefferson. I saved this for last because it's so boring."

Adam's body stiffened.

"What's that??"

Doctor Hansen: "What is it Adam?"

"There was a loud sound somewhere out in the warehouse. It sounded like someone dropping a tool, like a wrench or something. I'm looking at dad and he's looking at me. Dad's stepping out of his office and looking from left to right."

"He's coming back."

"What is it dad?"

"Dad's not answering."

"He's going in his desk for something."

Adam's breathing became heavy as he gripped both sides of the chair.

"It's a gun!"

Doctor Hansen: "Tell me what you're feeling right now."

"I'm scared. I never saw dad holding a gun before. Why does he need it?"

Doctor Hansen: "What's going on now?"

"Dad's telling me to hide behind the desk and be as quiet as a mouse while he goes walking around to check out the warehouse. Dad said it's probably nothing, but told me not to move. I'm hiding behind a big desk looking out from underneath and I see dad's legs walking out of the door. I don't want to stay here. I'm scared."

Doctor Hansen:  "Go on Adam, tell me what happens next."

"Dad's been gone for a long time. I don't like lying on this cold, hard floor. I'm crawling out from under the desk and walking out of the office to go look for him. Where is he? Dad, I'm scared. Where are you?"

"I'm whispering for him, but he doesn't answer. It's a big warehouse, so maybe he doesn't hear me. I keep walking and then...."

Doctor Hansen:  "Go on Adam, what then?"

"Finally! There he is!"

"I see dad standing like a statue. I've never been to this part of the warehouse before. What is he looking at?"

"He's looking at something and he has his arms out like he's trying to stop something. I can't see what it is because it's blocked by a wall."

Doctor Hansen: Can you see what's behind the wall?

Adam started breathing heavier and beads of sweat formed on his forehead.

"I'm slowly walking around dad so I can see what he's looking at. I'm trying not to make any noise. I'm pretty close to him, but he doesn't see or hear me. I continue walking around the wall. I see it now. He's looking at another man. The man is pointing something at him, but the man and dad aren't talking."

"What is that man holding?"

Adam let out a shriek that jolted everyone in the room.

"It's dad's gun! How did the man get it?"

"DAD, WATCH OUT!"

Doctor Hansen: "It's OK Adam. I'm here with you. Tell me what's happening now."

"I screamed and I scared both of them. Now the man is pointing the gun at me. Dad runs and pushes me really hard, and I'm falling backwards."

"OW!"

"My head hit something really hard."

"I'm seeing stars."

"I think something broke because I hear a loud pop. I'm opening my eyes. Now I'm sitting against the wall. I feel something warm and wet running down my neck. I'm looking up and I see dad on his knees with his head hanging down. Dad's falling. Everything is slowing down. What's happening?"

Doctor Hansen: "Go on Adam. It's OK."

"There's a small spot on the back of dad's shirt, and it looks like it's growing. It's red now and still growing. It looks like a leaf growing on a tree."

Adam slowly loosened his grip on the chair as his breathing became shallower.

"I'm feeling dizzy. Everything is getting dark. I'm so tired...."

Doctor Hansen: "Adam, listen to my voice. I'm going to count backwards from five to one."

"At one, you'll open your eyes."

"5...4...3..."

"You feel the weight of your body returning and you're no longer afraid..."

"2...1.."

"Open your eyes now."

Adam slowly opened his eyes and blinked. He was back in his grandmother's house surrounded by his grandmother, his mother, and Dr. Hansen. The room was still dark, and the lamp was still on, with the lava now flowing faster than before.

Dr. Hansen leaned in closer to Adam.

"How do you feel?"

Adam was trying to gather his thoughts for what seemed like an eternity.

"Dad was killed last year at his job. I remember everything now," answered Adam, finally.

His mother rose from her chair, walked over to him, and hugged him with tears running down her face.

"It's OK Adam. You're OK. We can all heal now."

She looked back at Dr. Hansen and silently mouthed the words "Thank you."

Adam got up and walked over to his grandmother. They all embraced and cried in the still darkness of the room as Dr. Hansen quietly packed her bags and left.

150

# Chapter

# Sixteen

*I*t was early Sunday afternoon, and both Adam and his mother had a long drive back to Somberville ahead of them. His mother finished packing up their things and loaded up the car. Adam sat with his grandmother talking. The weather was sunny and brisk as they helped his grandmother to the car. Adam's mother checked inside the house one more time to make sure they didn't forget anything. She lingered in the doorway for a while, remembering all the fond memories of her childhood. "It would be a shame to sell this house," she thought to herself. Finally, she switched off the hallway light, closed the door, and climbed into the car.

They all sat in the car staring at the house in silence. Eventually, Adam's mother turned around and broke the silence.

"Mom, I'd like you to come live with us in Somberville. I've already talked to the staff at Cedar. I just have to fill out some paperwork and it's done. We can come get you by next weekend. We should get some money from Martin's job, so we can get you the best in-home care. Will you say yes?"

Grandmother thought for a moment before eventually nodding in agreement and smiling.

Adam looked over at his mother curiously. He wondered what money she was talking about, but didn't want to ask in front of his grandmother. They started the car and left for Cedar Retirement Home. During the short drive, she looked over at Adam several times.

"Adam, I know all of this is hard to take in, but I want you to know that we're going get you someone to talk to regularly. You can always talk to me too. You know that, right?"

Adam didn't answer, but watched the buildings speed by. She looked over at him again.

"Adam?"

"I'm OK," he answered, still staring out of the window.

"It's kind of hard to explain, but I feel better. I used to think I was starting to have a headache if I stared at something for too long, but now I don't feel that way."

Then he turned to his mother.

"Can we go see him? At the cemetery I mean."

She smiled and reached over to stroke his hair.

"Of course we can Addy."

In what seemed like no time at all, they arrived back at Cedar Retirement Home. They unpacked grandmother's belongings and walked into the building. They arrived after the lunch hour, but Adam's mother convinced the staff to warm up something for the three of them to eat. As they were eating a late lunch, they talked about the future. They talked about finally selling grandmother's house, to which she agreed. Adam's grandmother held his hand the entire time they were at the table. After eating, they said goodbye to her and stopped at the front desk. She made sure everything was set for his grandmother's move the following weekend.

As they walked back to the car, Adam asked, "What did you mean about the money from dad's job?"

"Well, it's a pretty long and complicated story, Addy," she answered.

"When those things happened last year, the supervisors tried to blame it on your father. They argued that it was irresponsible for him to leave his post during his break to come pick you up from school, even if only for ten minutes. Those miserable bosses tried to blame everything on your father, saying he probably left the doors unlocked when he went to pick you up. They have never been able to prove that, but they were really fighting the insurance company over it. I had to hire a lawyer to straighten things out. We fought with them for almost a year, but we finally won. Your father's old company will be giving us money very soon and it will make life a little bit easier for us. Understand?"

"I think so," Adam began.

"What ever happened to that man? Did they catch him?"

"Yes they did. One of the cameras at the warehouse took a picture of his face and it was all over the news. He's going to be in jail for a very long time. One of the reasons that I wanted us to leave was because the TV news crews were constantly in front of our house. I was desperately trying to protect you from all of that before you got home from the hospital."

The cemetery was at the end of a long, winding rural road. They had stopped at a local store to pick up fresh flowers. Adam had been to this cemetery before to visit his grandfather's grave, but that was years ago. They slowed down at the top of the hill that overlooked most of the cemetery. There were tombstones of all shapes and sizes ranging from the size of a football to the size of a refrigerator.

They walked up the hill where the number of tombstones became sparser. Up in the distance, Adam could see a medium sized tombstone with a patch of soil in front that seemed fresher than the others. As they walked around the tombstone, his heart started beating faster. He squinted in the sunlight that was now facing them. Nevertheless he could now see the words inscribed on the tombstone:

*'Here lies Martin Dunne. Beloved husband and devoted father. Born April 20, 1973 – Died September 5, 2013.'*

Adam's mother held his hand as she brushed off the leaves that had fallen on and around the tombstone. Up to this point, the death of his father seemed surreal to him.

He turned to face his mother.

"Mom, I have to tell you something.  I've been talking to dad almost every night. He comes to my room, and we talk for a long time. Does that mean he's a ghost now?"

She didn't seem shocked by his confession.

"Well, Addy, our brain sometimes works in strange ways. Sometimes we see and hear what we want to see and hear. They say that there's no such thing as ghosts, but I'm not so sure. Sometimes when I sit with my eyes closed, I can sense your father there. I can even smell his cologne. Your dad will always be watching over us. I think he visited you to help you when you needed help. When you woke up from your coma, you had no memory of what happened. The doctors called it amnesia, but deep down I think you just blocked it out of your memory as a defense mechanism. Maybe your father helped you through it."

They placed the flowers in front of the tombstone and his mother said a short prayer. As they walked back to the car, Adam looked back at the grave and wondered if his dad was watching. As they sat back in the car, she turned the key and looked at her watch.

"Do you still feel like seeing your friend Philip? Maybe it's still too soon for you," she said.

"No, it's okay. I want to," answered Adam.

"Okay, let me give his mother a call to let her know we're on our way," she said, reaching in her purse for her phone.

Philip lived near the center of town close to Adam's old house. As they drove through the neighborhood, Adam felt as if he had never left. There was Peppy's Pizza, where he and parents would go on special occasions.  There was Lingstrom's Books, the bookstore that was always on the verge of going out of business, but somehow never did. He and Philip used to hang out there for hours at a time, reading until getting kicked out for treating it like a public library. There was Supreme Ice Cream, where he and his father would often secretly pig out on the flavor of the month. Finally, they arrived at Philip's house.

Adam looked up and saw Philip at the window looking out for them. As they were getting out of the car, Philip opened the door and stood in the doorway. He held up his hand as if afraid to wave. Adam held up his hand in response and walked up to the door. Philip's mother appeared behind him and opened the door wide.

"Hi Linda. Hi Adam. It's so nice to see you. Come on in."

Philip greeted Adam with "Hey," to which Adam responded likewise. With this single, simple greeting, Adam immediately understood that Philip knew the whole story. Therefore, the customary insult was inappropriate.

"We were just going to sit down for dinner. Will you join us?" asked Philip's mother.

Adam and his mother looked at each other and both agreed considering they had a long drive ahead of them. They sat down at the dining table talking about old times and what had happened in Melba within the last year. Adam's mother was careful not to bring up Adam's session with the doctor. She simply told them that Adam's memory had returned. After dinner they continued to talk until Philip got up from the table and beckoned Adam to follow him outside. The two of them sat down on the steps, and Philip for once didn't really have much to say.

"So you're okay now?" Philip asked, rather clumsily.

"Yeah, I'm okay. Mom says I still have to talk to people about my feelings or whatever, but I feel okay."

"You guys left so suddenly. You were in the hospital for a while, and then you just left. You were in a coma. How was that?" Philips asked.

He then realized it was silly question and corrected himself.

"I mean, do you remember anything while you were in a coma?"

Adam thought for a moment.

"No, I just remember waking up with my mom sitting beside me and things beeping."

"I did come and see you once," Philip said.

"It was weird because it just looked like you were sleeping. I brought that Tesla book that you let me borrow. I didn't understand anything."

"Hey, did you like the bookmark, by the way?" Philip added.

Adam looked at Philip curiously.

"What bookmark?" he asked.

"The 'Freak' bookmark? I even wrote it on shiny paper. You mean you never got it?"

Adam looked down remembering the paper that fell out of his book, and smiled.

"Yeah, I got it…. Butthead."

They both laughed and talked about some of their old friends and what they were up to until the sun started to set. After a while, Adam's mother came outside.

"Well Adam, I think we should hit the road. It'll be dark soon. I told Philip's mother that we'll be back next weekend, and they can visit us anytime."

Adam and his mother said their goodbyes and drove off. Adam's best friend was standing on the doorstep waving until Adam's car was out of sight.

# Chapter

# Seventeen

*T*he sun was down as they entered the highway. Adam's mother was quiet for the first 30 minutes of the trip.

"Adam, I never asked you how you felt about staying in Somberville," she finally said, touching Adam's shoulder.

Adam thought about his old friends and how much he missed them. But he also thought about the bookmark and how it seemed to change his outlook about his new home.

"No, I like Somberville," he finally answered.

"Oh, I'm so happy to hear that," his mother said smiling.

"I was so worried about it. You know, you can take some time off from school if you want to. I'll be quitting work at the diner so we can take some time together to relax. What do you think?"

Adam pondered the question for a while.

"No, I wanna go to school tomorrow," he answered.

"Okay, it's your choice. It'll be okay if you decide to change your mind and need time. I don't mind quitting my job because I must say that it is the worst job I have ever had. And the shift hours are terrible too, as you know. I always come home with my feet and back hurting. I feel bad that you're spending so much time alone. I get home so late when you're already in bed. We should be able to take long vacations together whenever you have school breaks."

"It looks like things will change for the better from now on," she added with a certain confidence in her voice.

During the rest of the trip they talked about the funniest memories of Adam's father. Adam remembered the time that he and his father built a birdhouse. Adam had the job of painting the house, but he used red watercolor instead of red acrylic. Whenever it rained, birds flew into the house as sparrows, and exited as cardinals. They talked about the time that a squirrel got into the house, making his mother run around screaming while his father chased the squirrel around with a tennis racket. There was also the time when Adam tried to make pancakes for his father on Father's Day. What he ended up making was something that looked more like hockey pucks, but his father ate them anyways, pretending that they were the best pancakes ever.

As the car entered the outskirts of Somberville, Adam's mother noticed that Adam was dozing off.  She looked at her watch that showed 10:20pm.

She thought that it would be just enough time to unload most of the stuff, grab a quick bite to eat, and head straight to bed. When they pulled up in front of their house on Pine Street, the sudden lack of motion jolted Adam awake. He looked around scratching his head and realized that they were home. The street was already dark. There were only a few lights on inside the houses, since people in Somberville weren't exactly night owls.

Adam's mother sat staring at the dashboard, then turned to Adam.

"Addy, I need to say this and hear me out."

Adam wasn't quite sure what she was about to say, so he looked down and mentally prepared himself.

"I'm really, truly sorry for what I put you through over the past year. While you were in the hospital there was a swarm of TV news crews around our house. They were relentless and just wanted a story and didn't care how they got it, or how we were suffering. I was already dealing with your grandmother at the same time and was arranging her care. Philip's mother helped me through it and also helped me arrange your father's funeral."

She wiped away her tears.

"I was at the hospital every day while you were in a coma and it broke my heart to see you in such a condition. It was complete chaos and the TV news crew simply would not go away. I vowed that there was no way they would get near you."

He looked over at her as she spoke, and noticed her trembling.

"Then, miraculously you woke up. I was asleep in the chair in your room and I hear you call for your father. I screamed for the doctors and nurses who then rushed into your room and examined you. After we figured out that you had no memory of what had happened, I thought it was both a blessing and a curse."

"I came home really excited to have you back, and I went home with boosted spirits. That same day the TV news crew cornered me in front of our house, shoving cameras in my face. I screamed at them at the top of my lungs and shoved them out of my way. That day I made up my mind that enough was enough. I boxed up a lot of things, stored them in your grandmother's basement, and sold the rest. When they cleared you to be released, I packed up everything that I could fit into the car. I arranged so that you would be discharged from the hospital at night. I came and got you late at night and got on the highway and just drove."

She brushed her hair back nervously.

"At the beginning I thought I was protecting you, but as time went on it was more like I was protecting myself. I would hear you in your room at night talking to yourself. I just told myself that you would be ok, and that you just needed time. Before I knew it, a year went by and I could see things weren't getting any better."

As she talked, she wiped her tears from her face again and put her hand over his.

"I didn't mean to make this harder on you, Addy."

"It's ok mom. I understand. I don't blame you," Addy finally answered, grabbing her shoulder.

She suddenly burst into full tears and started sobbing.

They sat in front of their house on Pine Street in an embrace, until she finally took a deep breath.

"You're such a brave boy. I don't know what I'd do without you."

Adam tried to think of something clever to make her feel better.

"You'd probably be eating your own meatloaf."

They stared at each other for a few seconds until they both spontaneously started laughing. Wiping away the remainder of her tears, she kissed him and finally opened the car door.

"You're such a wise guy."

They unpacked a few essential things from the car and headed into the house. Since Adam wasn't that hungry, he only ate a few nibbles from last week's leftover cold pizza, then went to bed. After she kissed him goodnight and turned off the light, he lay there for awhile, waiting to see if his father would appear. After waiting and watching the clock for 30 minutes, he thought that maybe his father would not show himself again. Even worse, perhaps it was his imagination the whole time. He turned over, closed his eyes, and drifted off into a deep sleep.

The slightly open window was letting in the cool air and a breeze gently stroked Adam's hair as he peacefully slept.

# Chapter

# Eighteen

*H*e knew it was just a dream, but this time he felt different about it; the fear and anxiety was no longer there.

Adam's old room in Melba faced the narrow creek that ran behind his house.  He looked out of his window and saw his father standing outside with his back turned. Although it was the middle of the night, he could tell that his father was wearing his favorite black jacket with a torn pocket. Adam walked downstairs and out of the back door wearing only his pajamas. As he approached his father, snow began to fall. He looked up and saw millions of snowflakes wafting through the air. He held out his hand to catch a few and found that they weren't cold. In fact, it reminded him of feathers flying through the air after a pillow fight. Adam continued to walk towards his father who was still standing off in the short distance with his back turned.

As he got closer, Adam expected to see the red leaf, but this time he saw nothing but snow covering his father's black jacket. He noticed that his father was staring straight ahead and to the left. The small creek had somehow disappeared. Instead, the ground continued on into hills that weren't there before. Now Adam stood directly behind his father, working up enough courage to speak.

"Dad, where did those hills come from? They weren't here before."

His father turned around and smiled, but said nothing. Without a word, he started to walk towards the hills. Adam looked up into the hills where his father was headed. There were hundreds of rows of small houses with glowing lights shining through the windows. All the lights were flickering candles and they seemed to be the only source of illumination in the vast darkness. To Adam, the entire scene seemed like something from a Christmas card. He followed his father, walking slowly behind him. He didn't feel cold, but rather warm as if walking through his grandmother's living room with the cozy fireplace blazing.

His father followed a path leading further up into the hills and Adam continued to follow him, looking at each house along the way. As much as he tried, he could see no people inside of them. The falling snow was becoming thicker now, but Adam kept an eye on his father, closely following behind him.

His father turned left onto a path and Adam turned with him. Adam looked back and saw that although they had only been walking for a few minutes, his house was now far down in a valley.

"Dad, where are you going?" he called out.

His father didn't answer, but he continued to walk as if knowing the route by heart. He made a right and continued upward. further into the hills.  Adam followed ten steps behind throughout the trek. Off in the distance and through the thick snow, he could see a huge building that resembled a concert hall of some sort. The light from this building's windows was much brighter than the surrounding houses, and it seemed to make the effect of daylight around it. Adam's father walked towards this building as Adam finally caught up to him.

His father stopped in front of the massive door and turned around to face Adam.

"Adam, this is as far as you go," he said softly.

He knelt down to Adam's level and put his hand on his shoulder.

"Adam, I didn't mean to deceive you. Neither did your mother. We have to accept things in our own way, and as mom told you before, it had to be your journey. Nobody could make it for you."

"Will I ever see you again?" Adam asked.

Adam's father smiled.

"You'll see me even when you don't. I'll always be with you."

Adam had always been confused by his father's riddles, but this time he knew exactly what he meant.

"Everything will be OK. You'll see," added his father.

Then he stood up, and at that moment the doors of the hall began to open. The light coming from within was blinding, but his father stared right into it and walked towards it. Adam watched as his father entered the building, turning his head one last time to smile back at him. Then the doors closed behind him and everything went dark. Adam turned around and saw that the hillside was now completely dark and it was starting to get cold.

He began to walk back towards his house, but soon lost his way. He tried to follow the tracks in the snow, but saw only a single set of tracks belonging to him that were rapidly being covered with snow. He tried to find his house down in the valley, but the snow had now become so thick that it was impossible to see.

Gradually, the snow seemed to fall much slower until it suddenly stopped in midair. He reached out his hand and grabbed one of the snowflakes. He held it in the palm of his hand. To his surprise, the snowflake did not melt, but remained in his palm generating a warm feeling. It appeared to emanate a tiny glow as if it was alive. Without warning, the snowflake floated back up into the air. Adam looked around and saw that all the snowflakes were now flowing upward back into the sky. At that moment, his body started to feel weightless and he felt his feet leave the ground along with the snowflakes. Before long he was floating over the hillside looking down at the houses that became increasingly smaller. He didn't continue to follow the upward direction of the snowflakes, but took his own path floating over the valley.

Off in the distance, the shapes of buildings came into focus and he began to recognize them many of them. He saw his old school and the playground where he used to play. He saw the empty parking lot where he first learned how to ride a bicycle, which led to his horrific crash. The feeling that swathed his body was utter bliss and he wondered if this was what it felt like to die and go to heaven. For nearly a year he had dreaded going to sleep, not knowing what demons would be waiting for him. This time, the feeling of anxiety and dread was gone, and what remained was nothing but harmony. He tried to look back towards the huge building that he and his father walked to, but could only see darkness behind him.

At last, Adam could make out his old house in the distance. Without really trying, he found that he was able to direct himself toward his house just by focusing on it. He could see that the back door was still open, as if waiting for him. Without a sound, he landed softly on the ground. Looking around while entering his house, he could see no lights on in the neighbor's houses. He walked upstairs and climbed into bed, never taking his eyes off of the window. As he lay there, he realized that all of the snow had disappeared, revealing the bright full moon.

172

# Chapter

# Nineteen

*T*he next morning Adam felt very energetic. He literally jumped out of bed, quickly got dressed, and ran down the stairs. His mother was already in the kitchen drinking her coffee, with breakfast already prepared for him.

"Wow, you're in good spirits today," she said as she looked up from her morning paper.

"I guess I slept okay," he said.

"No bad dreams?" she asked.

"No, actually I think I remember dreaming that I was flying. I'm so hungry," he answered as he pulled the plate closer and began to eat.

Adam decided to keep the rest of his dream to himself. He finished his breakfast and stared at the pill beside his glass of orange juice. He started to reach for it, but his mother covered the pill with her hand.

"Why don't you try a day without it?" she said smiling.

It was unusual for her to suggest not taking his pill, and the thought of going an entire day without his special headache pill made him a little nervous. He finished his juice and his mother gave him a longer than usual hug and kiss at the front door.

"Remember, if you feel the smallest headache coming on, have the school nurse call me immediately. Do you understand?"

Adam agreed. He left home at the usual time and started walking through his zones to school. Adam kicked through the leaves in his path that had fallen from the increasingly barren trees. The houses along the way were all decorated with corn stalks and paper turkeys hanging from the doors. Adam realized that he hadn't really done much with his Thanksgiving project that was due in one week, but he didn't care. As he breathed, steam billowed from his mouth. The days were getting even colder and he knew that it meant that the holiday season was approaching, which made him realize that Thanksgiving and Christmas would be spent without with his father, only this time it wouldn't be because he was too busy working or in class. The thought of it made him sad and his pace to school started to slow down. He wondered if his father would ever visit him again, perhaps in his dreams. Did the revelation mean that his connection to his father was broken forever? Adam tried to think of something else to take his mind away from this terrible thought.

Off in the distance he heard the first school bell ring, which meant he had exactly five minutes to get to class. He picked up his pace again and finally reached the school grounds. There, a red haired girl in a red dress was standing at the gate looking out. It was Melissa.

"Adam!" she called out waiving. "I was waiting for you. How was your weekend?"

Adam paused, trying to find an answer that didn't sound strange. Finally he looked away and decided to tell her the truth.

"Melissa, I told you on Friday that my father was going with us. That was a lie. My father died last year," he confessed, still trying to avoid direct eye contact.

"I know," answered Melissa.

Adam looked at her with surprise.

"How did you know?"

Melissa stepped closer.

"My mother told me. Remember me telling you that she worked at the news station? I guess she couldn't forget that she had seen your mom somewhere, and then remembered it was on TV. She went through some old news videos at her job and saw that your mom was on the news last year. I'm really sorry, Adam."

In the short time between the first and second school bell, Adam told Melissa of his weekend which seemed like a lifetime to him. He told of the trip to Somberville and meeting his grandmother. He told of his horrifying dreams. He revealed the details of his session with the doctor, who helped assemble the missing pieces of his memory. Melissa listened intently, but was more struck by the fact that this was the most that he had ever spoken aside from his oral report.

At the end of his story, Adam told her that he missed his father.

Melissa searched for words to make Adam feel that he was not alone.

"I had a cousin," Melissa started.

"Her name was Heather. We were like sisters. We did everything together. One day I noticed that Heather started to get really tired, only after me being at her place for a short time. At first, I just thought she was pretending and she just didn't want me around anymore. I remember I got really mad. She started to take naps during the day. Then one day, her mother told me I couldn't visit anymore. I was sitting in my room and my parents walked in and told me that Heather had leukemia. I didn't know what that was at the time, but I remember I was so scared that I might have done something wrong to make her get it. Before long, we had to go to the hospital to visit her. I remember that each time we visited her she looked less and less like my cousin. She was so skinny and pale, and had all these tubes inside of her. To this day I hate going to the hospital for anything because it reminds me of that time. Well anyway, one day I was in class and my mom appeared at the door. She looked really sad, and I just knew."

Adam looked at her with empathy.

"I guess that's the first time I experienced someone close dying." she added.

Melissa grabbed Adam's hand and gave him a look of compassion.

"You have to walk through the tunnel to get to the light."

Adam had a look of disbelief.

"Wow."

She looked at him curiously.

"What? My dad always says that."

Adam realized that she repeated those exact words from his dream that she was in, but in the end he decided not to mention it.

"Nothing. Never mind. It was just déjà vu."

Together they walked into the building just as the second bell rang. As they walked through the hallway heading to their class, Adam realized that he had forgotten his Tesla books at home.

But for once, he thought, it wasn't so bad.

179

180

181

# THE END